# MERITOCRACY

# MERITOCRACY

## A LOVE STORY

A NOVEL BY

JEFFREY LEWIS

Other Press • New York

Jacket photo: Gayle Lewis

Production Editor: Robert D. Hack

Text Designer: Natalya Balnova

This book was set in Caslon 540 by Alpha Graphics of Pittsfield, NH.

10 9 8 7 6 5 4 3 2 1

Library of Congress Cataloging-in-Publication Data

Lewis, Jeffrey.
    Meritocracy : a love story, a novel / by Jeffrey Lewis.
        p. cm.
    ISBN 1-59051-142-5 (hardcover : alk. paper)
    1. Vietnamese Conflict, 1961–1975—Maine–Fiction.   2. College graduates—Fiction.   3. Male friendship—Fiction.   4. Summer resorts—Fiction.
5. Maine—Fiction.   I. Title.
    PS3612.E965M47 2004
    813'.6—dc22
                                                                              2004002986

# CHAPTER 1

It was six hours from Boston to where we were going. It rained from Augusta to Belfast, and then along the coast road there were patches of fog. After Bucksport we turned off Route 1 and the road became narrow and roughly repaired and it roller-coastered up and down the hilly country. We passed a blueberry packing plant lit like an all-night truck stop and closed garages and repair shops and empty black farmland, and I began to feel a cool unease in my throat and in the tips of my fingers, not for the passing scene but for the fact that we were getting closer. Just as now, half a lifetime later, when the potholed road and astral blueberry plant dot my memory like so many fossils from an otherwise eroded landscape, I feel on beginning to tell this story a sense of trespass, as if what happened that weekend is none of my business, and never was.

I didn't own a car then. I had no money. I was a scholarship kid from Rochester and I'd never been to Maine and my ideas of it were taken from old ViewMasters. Three of us drove up in the metallic blue F-85 Cutlass convertible that Teddy's parents had given him, on no particular occasion, no birthday, not even a B+ on a Milton paper, sometime in his junior year. Cord lay across the backseat with his face in his balled-up Shetland sweater as if it were a roadtrip back from Vassar. In the argot of the time it was road shortener that had put him in this state, road shortener meaning beer. I wonder sometimes what happens to clever slang, whether literature becomes its museum or it just gets buried in the ground like the ruins of cities, awaiting chance rediscovery by the next generation of sarcastic kids. "Road shortener" I haven't heard in decades. Cord roused himself mainly to piss, or to provide sudsy tour-guide commentary, about lobster stands and the locales of failed trysts and the size of a full-grown monster moose and about the place we were going, where his family had their compound, that it was called Clements Cove, or Clement's Cove, or Clements' Cove, the locals had been fighting over the apostrophe for a hundred fifty years, long after the last of the Clements or Clementses were gone from the coast. This was the weekend past Labor Day, in the summer of our graduation, in 1966. Harry and Sascha had been married in June. They were driving up separately, and had gone to Bangor to pick up Adam Bloch, who took the bus. Harry was going in the army in a week. He wasn't even in ROTC. He was going as a grunt to Vietnam and this was the weekend we were sending him away.

All the rest of us had deferments, me to teach in Greece, Teddy for the Peace Corps, Cord for business school, Adam Bloch for grad school in economics. The normal run of things. Johnson was still president and there were still deferments to be had.

Everyone had an opinion as to why Harry was going to Vietnam, and I did too, but I never believed that I could get it all. My shortest version said Harry's father was the three-term senator from California and Harry was headed for politics and he knew it and the wisdom of the time was that if you wanted to go into politics you had to go in the service. It kept you alive anyway. If you dodged it you were dead. But the common phrase you always heard about Harry Nolan was what a crazy guy he was, and I was sure there was something more than politics to his decision, something macho or jocky, or one of those things we didn't talk about much because to talk about them was risking to kill them, duty or honor or whatever else. Better to leave it as Cord once said, that Harry'd rather have got himself shot at than go to graduate school. But none of us thought we knew it all, for instance how to figure Sascha, who hated his going, who would have gone in the Peace Corps with him, who married him regardless and in defiance. So maybe it came back, ninety percent anyway, to electoral viability, to the old man's advice. In the summer of 1966 it was still a little early to be way against the war, at least where we were. It was more something to be negotiated around, or if you were already in ROTC to be embraced with gritted teeth, or if you were Harry to say what the hell.

Teddy, I suppose, was one of a type who used to roam the east coast like wildebeests on the Serengeti, Greenwich, St. Grottlesex, his father big in advertising, a skinny guy with skinny tortoise shell glasses, silky dark hair, choirboy nose and lips and a neat backward part, someone you could imagine getting the epithet "fast" added to his name, like the guy who married Tricia Nixon, Fast Eddie whoever, forgotten now but there was a time around Harvard Law School and in *People* magazine when he was considered a fairly big cheese.

Teddy got us to Clements Cove in five hours instead of six. We stepped out of the fetid Cutlass into a moonless night so radiant it woke up even Cord. I was a city boy, unused to seeing a hundred thousand stars, and I wandered around like a dazed dim-wit until Cord said something like, "They got these things in New York?" "I know you think all Jews come from New York, but I actually grew up in Rochester." "In'nt that New York?" Ah yes, the old New York City/New York State conflation, cracker fuck-nose, I didn't say, because I didn't think of it but also letting Cord have the last word made me feel comradely. These were Harry's friends long before mine, his old, old friends, prep school and deb parties and summer places, and relative to all that I was still a new guy, roots no deeper than the spring grass. We un-loaded the trunk. We were parked on a sloping gravelly patch by Harry's old black Aston Martin. A few lights on here and there in the house. I couldn't tell much about the place, but that it was shingled and close by the water. I could hear the lapping of the bay. There were still a few mosquitoes and I waved them away, but no one else bothered.

A yellow bug light hung outside the kitchen door like the entrance to a quarantine area. Bloch was in the kitchen. "Can I help?" "Here, let me get that." "Any more out there?" Jesus, Bloch. His too-ready smile, his too-eager offers, his too-thick eye-brows. Can't you see we're grown men, we've got one bag apiece, no one said, because it was a weekend and he was Harry's latest find and we respected it and anyway you didn't cut people like Bloch directly, you cut them by looking past them, thanks any-way, got it covered.

Or it's possible Cord and Teddy didn't even notice that Bloch was annoying, maybe it was only me. What was Bloch doing here anyway? He wasn't my friend, he wasn't part of us, he was only Harry's friend. But of course Harry was the one going away. And without Harry I wouldn't have been here either. I wouldn't have known Cord or Teddy, I would have had different roommates entirely. And Sascha. Would I ever have heard her say my name, would I have more than seen her across a room or street, if not for Harry?

The main room was long with ceiling beams thicker than railway ties and an overscale stone fireplace that looked like the entrance to a cave. In all it resembled a ski lodge where somebody had gone through and taken out all the alpine motifs and replaced them with carved boats and nautical charts.

In front of the fireplace sprawled an ancient couch you could get lost in, deep-cushioned, floral-patterned, and Sascha was there, her knees up, Harry's crewcut head wedged against her, the rest of him across the couch like a dead guy. They were so loose-limbed, that was the thing. Or one of the things, anyway. Along with her dark restless hair, almost like a banner flying her name. And the embers of awareness in the center of her star-blue eyes, that seemed to say the world hadn't crushed her just when the world seemed to think it had. Her full lips, the slightly downturned corners of her mouth, a melancholy look, sleepless, complicated, a little bit cunning; a look of many cups of coffee, and somehow, always, injury without a mark. If her look was aristocratic, it was also not quite American, not all of it anyway. I hated superlatives then. They used to sound so stupid. But Sascha was my superlative. And Harry was my friend, and I was supposed to be his.

They didn't get up. Harry waved at us with a vague sweep of his hand, as though making fun of how little effort he would expend to greet us, how relaxed he was, how sweet life was this night. They'd started a fire, though the evening was only a little cool. The lights were out and the fire made shadow puppet play of their faces. Sascha smiled our way. She too waved, opening and shutting her fingers, and her brief smile was enough to lift the downturned corners of her mouth. I saw that much anyway, even if as a matter of self-preservation I was trying not to focus upon her too directly, was daring myself to see her as no more than a figure in a landscape.

We said a few things. It was mostly Cord who said them. Had they found something to eat? Were they warm enough? What time had they got here? Had they hit the construction on the bridge over the Kennebec? It was his family's place, his family's photos on the tables, and he had a southern way about him that was half gracious and half fussy, as he made his way around the room throwing switches and checking on the mice and whether the caretaker Everett had been into the Johnny Walker again. Cord's family were cotton farmers from Tennessee, which maybe meant plantation owners once, but they'd been sending their towhead boys north for Yankee schooling for enough years that there was an athletic trophy at Yale named after one of them and this compound had made its way into the family holdings. Cord had a faint, almost breathless voice, he spoke rapidly, he was by turns kind, malicious, and clowny, and it was sometimes hard to know which he was being because it was so hard to hear him. Long-limbed and big-handed, with stubbornly turned-up Nordic features, he seemed like one in whom the instinct to be just a big old farmboy, even after centuries of refinements and "good matches," had refused entirely to die. Cord was in every social grace sanded at least as smooth as Teddy, but take away the J. Press and cordovans and you could almost see a ghost draped over a plough.

It wasn't for me alone that Harry and Sascha were like a force field. Cord too, and Teddy, and Adam Bloch. All of us who were there that weekend, at one time or another, though Cord and Teddy wore their admiration lightly, more like peers of the realm. When I was in a room I was conscious of a part of me aimed in their direction, no matter which way I was facing. If they were apart, I was bifurcated, like an isosceles triangle. If I left the room, to go upstairs because Cord was going to show me where my room was, I felt a part of me tugging, left behind, like a character's foot in a cartoon mired in glue or pitch. These feelings diminished when I was away from them, though one or the other of them often came to my mind. I always felt the next time I saw them I wouldn't be so in their thrall. But it inevitably happened again, with as little as Harry's wave, as little as Sascha's complicated smile, which this night I was doing my best to avoid.

And beyond our little group I knew there must be others, in our class at Yale or Sascha's at Radcliffe or in Maine or Nantucket or New York or Virginia who loved the one or the other or both, or talked about how much they admired them when they too loved. I was a partisan, of course, a cheerleader of sorts, but why not? At the time I felt lucky to be close. It made my life make a kind of sense, just as two vectors aimed at the same point create the feeling we call fate.

Harry asked if we'd brought any beer and Cord said yes there was Carlings he'd put in the fridge but when Harry lifted his head off Sascha's lap she said "Don't go" and put her hand on him to stop him. Her voice was quiet then and frightened and sweet, a tiny diminished voice I'd never heard before. But in moments, after he kissed her lightly—just her lower lip he kissed—she let him go and he got up and that was the end of it, the end of her mocking herself on account of her fears or whatever it was. Cord and Sascha, who'd known one another longer than Harry had known her, because Sascha's sister Maisie had gone out with Cord's brother's roommate at Hotchkiss, chattered about Maisie wanting to transfer from Sarah Lawrence but she didn't know where, maybe Berkeley, get away from it all. Soon Harry was back and he and Sascha were as before and they drank a beer together. They were the last to come upstairs.

All of us slept up there, in a fairyland warren of rooms where the kids of Cord's family had been growing up for sixty years. My narrow bed was made up with a quilt and it creaked. There were camp pictures on the walls, all girls, and a yearbook from the Ethel Walker School on the painted bedside table. Outside was the dark of the bay, the starlight barely sprinkling it. For a long time I couldn't sleep because I was hearing Sascha's voice when she said "Don't go."

Teddy was the first up the next day and he'd found some eggs in the fridge and was making some weird egg dish that required putting the eggs in the oven with cheese on top of them. Shirred eggs à la something or other. He was darting around the country kitchen, he'd awakened with such a surplus of nervous energy it was as if he could have fried the eggs himself without a stove. I stood around and watched him a few minutes and went outside.

It was a gray morning that was cooler than the night before. The tide was coming in but it wasn't yet here, and I looked out on a landscape of mussel shells and black ooze, then the gray water looking cold and choppy beyond. The cove was cut deep and angular. On its far shore there were woods, a log cabin and a shingle cottage with a screened-in porch, a faded pier. Just outside the cove two bare islands sat, or maybe they were one when the tide was low. A rickety marker stuck out of the flank of one of them, tentative, annoying, like something a picador would stick in a bull. Cord's house was set right by the water. It too had a pier, which sagged then regained a little of its composure toward the end of it, like one of those hand bridges you see in *National Geographic* movies of Asia. The house itself sat on a shelf of rock, and at first I thought it looked brave and lonely, with its mottled brown shingles, but actually it wasn't so alone, this was a compound after all, and there were two more dark shingled houses visible through the spruce. They didn't look as big as Cord's. They belonged to other Elliotts, and then there was another shingled structure that looked like a shed. All this took money, I thought. The effect was not achieved without money, money as weathered as the shingles.

When I went back inside Harry was downstairs. He was in a white T-shirt and unshaved and he looked enough like Stanley Kowalski to give Brando fans pause. Harry was not one who'd ever bought into the idea of Ivy, or preppie for that matter when his parents sent him out of California to St. Paul's. Teddy still rode him about the surfboard he'd sent east and insisted on mounting like a dead shark over his bed. Harry was someone who wore anything his mother or a girlfriend bought for him, and now he'd married a woman who didn't shop at all. He was pretty much always down to a T-shirt and cutoffs, though occasionally a worn Lacoste would appear with the alligator falling off it. In a sense he was someone who didn't need clothes anyway. He had a thick neck and his jaw jutted and his forehead overhung his eyes, putting them in shadows. His body was something machine nouns stuck to, dynamo, turbine, Pratt-Whitney engine. He had hairy legs, his crewcut was pure Beach Boys, and in short he looked nothing like a Yale guy or even an eastern guy, he looked like a pure California guy, who'd only gone east because he'd been caught screwing the chaplain's daughter at Thacher, or maybe the thing about the chaplain's daughter was true but there was also noblesse oblige in there somewhere, even in California you went east to school if you were old money enough and didn't want to wind up a provincial moron. His full name, after all, was

Harry St. Christopher Nolan, the "St. Christopher" in grateful remembrance of a San Francisco department store fortune on his mother's side without which his father's rise in politics would have been as unlikely as Jack's on the beanstalk. So Harry had pedigree, even if he looked like a Marine recruit from Pismo Beach and talked with a soft twang, like a guy who missed the beach every day the surf was up.

"Hey." Now there was a word that Harry used a lot. A lot of the time it was the only word he used. It expressed acknowledgment. Everything else was optional. Usually friendly enough, that "Hey," but sometimes withheld, sometimes impatient, sometimes ridiculing, as though what really was meant was "Hey asshole" but he'd left off the rest of the sentence. "Hey Louie." That was me, that was good morning, that was how've you been since the wedding or whenever it was I last saw you. Harry sometimes forgot. Not the way most people forget such things, out of self-absorption, with Harry it was more like he'd been over-absorbed by the world. He remembered big emotions, he remembered bright divides, he remembered if somebody'd been a good guy or asshole. And he remembered—which I did not—jokes.

We ate our eggs standing up. Teddy had put in so much paprika he could have scorched the Hapsburg Empire. He seemed to think if it was good for deviled eggs, it would be good for whatever he was making. Nobody said anything. Teddy finally said how unbelievably fabulous he thought they were and we could just shove it if we didn't think so too, and in a pissy move was about to dump all the uneaten ones in the garbage, when Bloch walked in, wearing clothes too pressed for the country, his smile pleasant-enough now, face scrubbed. Neat. Bloch was always neat.

Teddy offered Adam breakfast. Would he like some shirred eggs, he could be the judge, he could be the neutral party, because some people thought they were less than fine. Bloch wasn't sure which way to flop on this. The one thing he knew for certain was that he didn't want to alienate anyone and that in this circumstance he could be considered the butt of a joke but on the other hand maybe it was good-natured and if he didn't play it that way everyone would think he was a flamer. He ate the eggs. Um good, Cord said. Fuck you, let Adam judge, Teddy said. I said nothing. I suppose I felt too close to Bloch's position. He took another bite. Not bad, he said. Pretty good, he said, and the rest of us managed not to laugh because we were so well brought up, but Bloch wasn't sure.

He mopped his plate clean with his toast. Maybe he really was just telling the truth, but Harry threw his out as soon as Teddy was gone and slugged orange juice to get the taste out and I did too. We passed the orange juice carton back and forth. Harry asked me how my summer had been. I felt again the warmth in the back of my neck and in my shoulders as though it were the gaze of the sun on me. I told him I'd been in Europe. Bumming around, got as far as Rome. Then came back to make some money because I was going away again in October. You lazy fuck, he said. Sascha walked in. She was wearing a man's shirt and her restless hair was pulled back by something. Before I could help it I'd looked at her. Not a half-look, unfocused, with others in the frame. I'd looked at her, and knew that I was still in love.

# CHAPTER 2

The year George W. Bush and Al Gore ran for president, it seemed like the whole country was clicking its tongue about them. The boys of privilege, the smirk and the lame, and everywhere the implication (if not the accusation) that this was the best our generation could produce, or at least that our elite could produce, our golden guys, who got into Yale or wherever and their mamas were pretty and they were pampered and raised up enough that their heads were over the clouds a little, so that they could see what was up better than the rest of us anyway, and to boot they were good-looking because their mamas were, and they had the money to get there. These. Ours. Mine. Another best and brightest story of going down in flames, the late-night comedians getting in theirs, a candidate whose most radical idea was abolishing the estate tax so that the rich could stay rich forever. And what did I think about it all? Mostly that the story was true, true as far as it went. But also I thought: *It ought to be Harry Nolan up there.*

One night I even dreamed of George Bush, in a moment of candor or nostalgia or even sweetness, saying the same thing. *It ought to be Harry Nolan up there, he's the one, he's a good man.* The way W. says "good man."

Bush was two classes behind us at Yale. He was in DKE. Harry was in DKE and he knew George pretty well and he liked him well enough, thought he was an okay guy anyway. But George idolized Harry. I know this because I saw it. George was in our rooms quite often in our senior year. I wasn't his friend but I knew who he was, mostly because Yale was like that then, you knew who was the son of somebody famous, and even then Bush the father was big in the Republican Party, running for the Senate or rising at the R.N.C., something like that. Like Harry, George was the son of somebody. They must have spotted each other on that basis alone from a half-mile off. That and DKE and the fact they were both preppies from the west. But Harry wouldn't have cared, he would simply have been aware, whereas with George I wouldn't know. All I knew was that he idolized Harry, that he would stand around our room silent in a varsity jacket with other DKEs watching Harry swat a squash ball against the wall or listening to his jokes or waiting on him to say any damned thing at all.

There were people who resented Harry Nolan, denigrated his athleticism, suspected his charm, denied his intelligence, thought the whole thing about him was a privileged brew of cult and hype; who hated California, hated jocky DKE though Harry hardly ever went over there, hated all the girls he screwed and that after screwing them he wound up with the Number One Girl of them all. It enraged them that more than anyone they knew or had heard of Harry Nolan was likely to wind up president of the country someday. They thought a person you could say that about, that he could or would be president, had to be a phony and a shallow piece of shit. But these, the haters, weren't many. He was too funny, too self-mocking, too wide-open and un-adorned. And he was one of those, in a class of a thousand, a college of four thousand, a university of ten thousand, everyone seemed to have heard of him. I probably could have counted a hundred people who knew me by my first name. Judging by the people who were always asking me about Harry, twenty times that number must have known him, because he'd drunk with them or driven them in his Aston or commiserated with them about one bit of horseshit or another or loaned them money or just because they did. If he crossed your path, you probably thought he liked you, and from that dared let escape the truth that preceded it and drove it, that your life's vote was his for the asking.

From our time at Yale there were a lot of guys who made it in politics. John Kerry who started prepping his run at the White House thirty years ago was in our class, and George Pataki of New York was the class after. And some Whitman in our class married Christie Todd to make Christie Todd Whitman, and of course there was Bush. And Joe Lieberman was two classes ahead of us, and John Ashcroft. At Harvard at the same time was Weld of Massachusetts, and Gore. And what year was it that Bill and Hillary entered Yale Law? I've never done the math. But it seems like a lot. The cream rising to the top, and then what?

Harry Nolan's name is not among them.

But getting back to Bush. Bush with his many flaws. My political views are perhaps what you'd expect, of a guy of a certain age, screenwriter, TV, briefly lawyer, bummed around, California, Europe, New York, an intellectual of sorts, a manqué of sorts. That is to say, I blame, I stew, I patronize, I write letters to the editor in my head, I cringe and take cheap shots and sometimes I despair. And yet, this evening in my chair, as for a little while I neglect his policies and remember the man, I'm having warmer feelings for George. He lies too much, of course. Clinton lied about sex but W. lies about virtually everything else, like a less-than-stellar candidate for mayor of Sheboygan.

But the way he tries to keep his head up, slightly stiff and meaningful, as if he's maybe afraid he isn't quite tall enough. Or for that matter the little thrusting of his chest when he thinks he's being filmed, when he's walking "official," like a stripper with new tits she's actually quite proud of. He seems, I suppose, such a simple, unguarded example of the way life challenges us all on an ongoing basis. A bit of dignity, perhaps. I keep thinking that might be what I'm seeing, growing, gaining firmness and fixity, out of the petulance and self-satisfaction. Or competing with them, anyway. Living side by side, peaceful coexistence. A boy who's trying, harder at times, less hard at others, to become a man.

It's just that he makes me think of Harry.

We used to say "good man," too. Harry did, a lot.

# CHAPTER 3

The cove wasn't a proper place for the Elliotts to keep their boat because of the mud at low tide, so we drove over to Bucks Harbor all stuffed into the F-85. Bucks Harbor was a pretty little cup of land almost stoppered by a dark green islet of spruce and pine that lay in the middle of its water. There was a tennis court with a falling-down fence and a low yacht club in the arts-and-crafts style and people from Philadelphia mostly were said (by Cord) to go there in the summer. Nice people, whitebread people, Protestant and Republican, they raced their sixteen-foot boats there and trained their kids to race their sixteen-foot boats and enjoyed the sweetness of life without the cares of time, long August days, but they were gone now. Bucks Harbor also had, up the shady road from the water, a general store, a white church, and Condon's garage, the last of which appeared, folksily drawn with its proprietor old man Condon, in a children's book by Robert McCloskey about a girl who lost a tooth. In the general store we bought sandwiches and drinks for our picnic.

There had been a hurricane warning the week before Labor Day and because of it many boats had been pulled and there were few in the water now. The Elliotts owned a Concordia but that had been pulled. On their mooring now was an aluminum skiff thirteen feet long with an outboard. We rowed out to it, half of us at a time, in a yacht club dinghy. I felt like a girl because I wasn't sure how to row even a rowboat and because it was Sascha who rowed Bloch and me and the bags of food out there. She had an easy, powerful stroke, her back arched, her slender arms supple and rhythmic, and we glided along in silence. Bloch was even more of a girl than I because he was afraid of the water and wore a life jacket, which he'd donned casually as though it were no big deal. Or this was how I thought about it anyway, as I sat there and was rowed like a young prince. I'd seldom been on salt water and the white curls of spray out past the islet gave me pause, but I wasn't going to wear a life jacket.

We were going to take the skiff out to one of the islands. The outboard was rust-old and cranky and Cord had to suck the gas out of the fuel line to prime it. He said it was that way when it was cold. The skiff was a tight fit for the six of us. It made for camaraderie, or at least something you could have taken a picture of and called camaraderie, standing up on the bow looking down at shivering smiles, but no one had a camera.

We came around the islet toward the harbor bell and the wind from down the Reach hit us and the flat aluminum hull banged on the water. Cord stood up in the stern and steered, his jaw a little into the wind as if he was auditioning for a shirt company's ad campaign. Sascha sat in the bottom of the boat in a green hooded sweatshirt with her knees up and Harry sat beside her holding a beer. Teddy hung over the bow like an overstimulated six-year-old claiming to be looking for porpoises. He was getting

soaked and his glasses were covered with spray but in a few minutes the porpoises came. There were three of them and they kept alongside of us and I felt like a city boy again because it seemed like such a miracle to me. They were small, gray porpoises and each time they dove they came up on the other side of us and at another angle, as if we were the center of a Minoan mosaic they were filling in. Then they were gone altogether. Teddy whapped the side of the boat with the flat of his hand, exhorted us with more sincerity than he sometimes showed in a month. "Come on. Everybody! Come *on*! They like that." So we all started doing it, even Sascha, whapping the aluminum sides as if they were drums and Cord cut the engine so the porpoises could hear our whapping better and wouldn't be frightened off.

But the porpoises didn't come back. It was a day the wind blew early, the sky was the creamy bright blue of a fifties convertible, and all along the waterline in every direction were the low wooded shapes of islands with the tide marks on their rocks.

The place we were going was called Crab Island, which was supposed to be on account of its shape but I couldn't see it. All I could see were trees here and there, trees everywhere really, and a couple of spindly points of land and a short pebbly beach. People went there for picnics because of the beach, Cord said, they'd been going there forever for picnics and the owner didn't mind. Turned out the owner was one of Sascha's uncles, Uncle James who bought islands. He had so many islands that he didn't visit them and they were left wild. The day was warming up, though the sun was pale now and beginning to be hazed over. There were rocks in the water as we approached the beach and we were all supposed to lean over the side and look out for them and Adam Bloch made a big officious deal of looking out for them but didn't see any. Cord cut the outboard. We could see the bottom now. Harry jumped into the dark water, which swallowed him to his waist. He yelped facetiously for how frigid it was and pulled us ashore.

Sascha held her moccasins and slipped down into the ankle-deep water. There was something so easy and natural about her she very nearly left nothing to describe. A man is badly advised to want to describe a cloud or a god. Sascha had the gift of seeming to occupy only the space that belonged to her, only the parts of life she needed. Whereas I for example seemed in my damning comparison always to be leaping out of myself, stretching even when I didn't need to, involuntarily, and Cord, too, with his manners and whole sentences and Teddy with his jumpy Connecticut sarcasm. Sascha had shadows, but they were sharp and real, as sharp and real as she was. Maybe she was just too rich to bother putting on a show. She was not a theatrical person, she was one who would take in a performance, not give it. Yet Cord was rich, and Teddy was rich, by any ordinary mortal's standard. Or we all were, if you stopped and looked at the world. She seemed, walking ashore, walking the beach in her bare feet looking down, not just rich but a little fatigued by it, by all that surrounded her, and so she was left without the means to make anything up.

Late adolescent scales of judgment, full of bright lines. And where did Harry fit? He walked beside her on the beach and there was nothing wrong with the picture. He walked like a consort of an end-of-the-world perfection, like Indian gods both of them, like Shiva with Parvati.

Or am I bringing up old insanities now, do I give myself-that-used-to-be away?

I was eager to be liked and they weren't. Maybe that's all it was.

We had our picnic on the beach. Bloch sat on his life jacket and absorbed potshots from Teddy for needing his ass to be comfy. We ate sandwiches and cookies and finished most of the beer. Sascha drank a canned ice tea. As if she weren't there, as if he'd landed for a moment in a different weekend, Harry got onto a riff about Willie McCovey. "The highest slugging percentage in the majors." "McCovey's a maniac." "McCovey's a god." "No disrespect to Mays, Mays is Mays. But it's McCovey you want in the clutch." A San Francisco monologue, punctured only by Teddy who was a Yankees and Mantle guy, but the Yankees weren't in it that September and the Giants were. McCovey, Mays, and Marichal. Marichal, McCovey, and Mays. "And don't forget a little name like Jim Ray Hart." Jim Ray who? We were like seals sunning ourselves. Once or twice on the way over we'd seen lobster boats in the distance, but now there were no boats out.

It is a day the Lord hath made. Cord was always saying that. Sometimes sardonic, sometimes enthused. And as for Sascha and Harry, on short time together, you could look at them and almost forget that it was going to happen. Why should it? The breeze was sweet against her hair. Harry had his Giants in the race. And anyway it wasn't quite the end of the string yet, Harry didn't have to be in Oakland until Friday and on Monday they would leave Clements Cove and drive farther along the coast to her family house on Mount Desert, where they would spend their last days alone. Sascha wasn't teary or morose, they didn't seem to have to be with each other every moment, they didn't even have that much to say to each other. They were simply there, as if it would always be that way until it wasn't.

On the other side of the island, Cord said, there was an old schooner whose owner had beached and burnt it there, and Harry wanted to see it. Sascha and I stayed behind while the others went.

I've told you that I loved her, but not that I had never done anything about it. I had been to their wedding. I had watched it all happen. I had watched it all happen all the way. And that wasn't going to change now. She had a book with her, something I didn't expect, an old best-seller with the dust jacket missing, the kind she might have found on a painted shelf in the room where they were staying. I tried again to look at her as little as possible, or anyway not so often that she'd notice. When I was with Sascha alone I felt myself turning at angles, as though to leave so thin a side of me turned to her that I wouldn't be seen, as though all of me was a private part to be covered up. She said something about it getting warm out. The others weren't back. She got up and took her sweatshirt off and laid the book on it. Sascha's voice was small like her mouth. She wasted few words, and what she said was unadorned. She said that she was going to take a walk.

Really, her words were like Shaker furniture. And what seemed like an afterthought, her asking me to come along.

We had been friends. When there were things about Harry, she had sometimes told me, "Louie, I want him to come with me to Cyprus this summer," "Louie, I have no idea what to get him for his birthday." Though I don't think she ever used me that way, telling me something she hoped would get back to him. She was too direct for that, as direct as a pole, really. I relegated myself to being her friend, kind, thoughtful, occasionally witty, the kinds of things that as a friend I could be. It let me see her anyway. It let me hear her voice addressed to me. What else could I do? And it kept me loyal to him, though my heart was not. My heart was in a turmoil; I accused myself all the time.

She put on her moccasins to walk. She was wearing the same men's shirt from yesterday. We walked along the beach and then onto a narrow path that climbed into the woods. It seemed like a path that rounded the island, staying just above the shore, and it was overgrown and rooted. I walked ahead of her, felt for a moment as if I were leading her. Somewhere in the woods she said to me, "Louie, do you think Harry's going to die?"

The kind of words that carry omen in them, but with Sascha they came out simply inquisitive. Did I have an opinion on this interesting topic?

"No," I said. "No, I don't. He'll probably fill sandbags for a year."

"I know there's a friend of his father. They want to make him a cameraman."

"Then he'll do that." Which, I felt, might put an end to it. A decent end, clarifying and reassuring. But I also felt a need to be the hero of the scene, so I added, "Harry's pretty tough. He loves you too much to get himself killed." Which as soon as I said it sounded trite and sentimental in the salt air of the island, to me at least, but maybe not to her.

"I hope so. You don't think he's just being a selfish jerk, do you, Louie?"

"No. You totally come first with him."

"Then I'm being the selfish jerk," she said.

"I wouldn't bet on that," I said, and her troubled eyes shot my way, like a bird landing on a branch.

"But Louie," she said, and in my fear of her I began to think she was playing with me, the way a parent keeps a baby going by calling its name. "Is any of it honest?"

"In what way? What do you mean?"

She'd picked up a stick and was lightly dragging the tip of it over the moss. "I don't know what I mean. Do you?"

I should have said no, of course I don't, how could I? But I felt honored by her asking, a sort of opportunity, as if a rabbi of Lublin had been invited to the king's court to talk about the stars. I asked, "Is it an honest reason for going? Is that what you're asking?"

"I guess. Yes. I think so."

"How could I know? I'm not even sure what his reason is."

"I'm not either. Isn't that the pits? I'm the wife."

"What does he say?"

"We don't talk about it anymore."

We walked along the path, came to a rivulet and crossed over.

You know what a wise man is? A boy who has no better way to be accepted. I gathered my words as if they were a precious harvest. "I guess the distinction would be if he's going because he believes it's his duty, or because he believes he has to be seen to be doing his duty."

"That's it," she said. "That's right." Though it wasn't like she said it with enthusiasm. She said it looking at the ground.

"I don't know," I said.

"I think you do. Louie, why do you diminish yourself?"

"Do I?"

"I think you do—maybe not always."

"About this, really, I don't know."

"I think the world's setting a trap for him and he's too something to avoid it."

"But what's the something?" I said, and although I still hadn't looked her way, I smiled sardonically, for the pleasure of our talk, the sound of her voice and my voice intertwined, her words wanting mine.

"You tell me," Sascha said, about the something. "Please. Just tell me. Even if it's not right, I want to think I understand."

"It's always two things with him," I said.

"But it's always one thing more than the other," she said.

We eventually came to where the others were poring over the burnt carcass of the schooner. There was hardly any of it left. It was split apart. It had been there forty years. People had stolen everything. It looked like dinosaur bones but it made Harry happy, he loved old wrecked things, maybe because he was from California where things were too new to be wrecked. Or that's too easy. I don't know. But when we got there Sascha came up to him, and he put an arm around her acceptingly, and she kissed him in an easy kind of way.

A little later we were back on the beach, skipping stones, hanging out. Sascha was lousy at skipping stones, and Harry was telling her to keep her arm down, to do it sidearm, but still her arm for this was weak, until at last she got one off, a little white stone that piddled on, five times, six times, it splashed and disappeared, and Harry winked at her and the rest of us said what a really good one it was.

"Why are you going?" Sascha asked. "Really."

She was looking for another stone.

"Going where?" Harry said, which he knew was not going to make it, since he added, "In the army?"

I thought it was odd, like a door flung open when there was no breeze for it. Didn't she mind that we were all there? It was as if she must want our help.

"Is it honor or hypocrisy?"

"Don't know what you're talking about."

"You do too."

Harry skipped another stone, he skipped it hard this time, a slatey jagged thing, and it banged nine or ten times on the water.

"For a lot of reasons. For one thing there's a draft in this country."

"You could get a deferment."

"A deferment's a deferment. You still have to do it later."

"Is that true?"

"Unless you want to keep doing stupid things until you're twenty-six," Teddy said.

"Harry. Really. I need to know."

"Whether it's honor or hypocrisy? Hypocrisy, obviously." He laughed like a horse and picked up a rock that was more like a boulder, that wasn't even flat, and he threw it at the water and it sank. "Fuck. . . . I mean, what do you even mean, Sascha? Really."

"Maybe they're the wrong words. Louie said it better. Louie, what did you say?"

Sascha being someone who didn't notice the spots she put other people in. Either she was too honest for it or she had never had to deal with consequences.

But in the end I didn't have to answer that one because once Harry's eyebrows knitted together and he felt challenged and sneak-attacked, he didn't hear much else but his own thunder.

"There's a draft in this country! Everyone's supposed to serve. These guys feel it too, they're doing something, for chrissake. Everyone does something. So this is what I'm doing. And do politics play a part in that? I have no idea. What can I tell you? Shooting guns is fun. I like shooting guns, I like camping out, I liked the Boy Scouts. Is that hypocrisy? What's hypocrisy?"

"Okay. Alright," she said, and it seemed like she had retreated.

But we all knew he had told her nothing, and I had the sick feeling that something I said only to win her approval and not even because I thought it was true, though it might have been true, had colored the afternoon.

We quieted down and finished whatever beer was left and then everyone snoozed for a little while or tried to. When I woke up, Bloch was sitting on his life jacket. He was staring toward where the bay opened wide to the southwest. Down there somewhere was Rockland. Cord had pointed it out, even if we couldn't exactly see it, and beyond Rockland the ocean. But all that was out there now was a fluffy low strip over the ocean the color of dirty snow.

"Is that coming our way?" I said.

"I don't know," he said.

"Is it fog?" I said.

"I don't know," he said.

But it was fog. I woke up Cord finally. I didn't want to be alarmist. But the fog was almost on us by then. Though we weren't going in its direction, it seemed like it would soon overtake us. That's what I guessed anyway, and it did.

We gathered our things together. The fog was such that we could barely see to where the boat was beached. Cord said once it was on us it could stay awhile. We didn't want to be stuck overnight on the island in the fog, so we left.

The thing about the fog was that we seemed so alone in it. It was as if the islands, the sky, the trees, the mainland across the bay, had simply deserted us. All at once they counted in the calculation of what was at some sharply discounted fraction, the exact number indeterminate, what you might use to count silent shades. We could have been in a play, six people stuck with our own footprints and voices.

And the other thing about it was that it distracted us from what had gone before. I felt the taint of my impure thoughts begin to dissolve in it. Though Harry was still quiet, ruminating, and I wondered what he was ruminating.

The feeble grinding of the three-horse outboard seemed tremendous now. For good measure, every minute or two I squeezed a foghorn that was about the size of a bicycle horn. It was a little like sending radio signals out into the cosmos. No boats honked us back. We really were alone.

Sascha sat in the bottom of the boat and tried to read her book. With his life jacket on and his blank, fixed expression Bloch looked like a soldier in a landing craft on D-Day. We went on this way for a time that became as hard to judge as distance. We distrusted Bloch's watch because it said only thirty minutes. Cord steered our little ship of fools, Teddy read out compass readings in ironic tones, Harry rubbed Sascha's feet to keep them warm.

I imagined it was only myself who had begun to wonder if we were going around in circles or if Teddy was sufficiently sober to read the compass or if the fog was ever going to lift or was it rather a half-assed clammy sign of evil out of a third-rate horror movie. Myself and Bloch, I imagined, but I didn't really include Bloch. He was like the second Jew aboard. I was the Jew in this boat. He was one too many Jews.

And where had he come from anyway? Pittsburgh, but where was that? Nowhere, out there somewhere, worse than Rochester even, at least if you were a Jew. The Mellons and the Pirates came from Pittsburgh, but who else? All the snob in me rallied against Bloch. Harry had met him in the Political Union. Harry had thought he was a really smart guy, an economics guy. Harry soaked up economics from Bloch the way he'd once in our freshman year soaked up Descartes and Leibniz and Kant from me.

Harry could see the role of Bloch, the need for Bloch, in future Nolan administrations, in future Nolan campaigns. You needed economic plans if you were going where Harry was going, and he was already getting prepared. Or that was my interpretation anyway, which left room for Harry not really to like Bloch, but rather simply to use him. I liked this because it meant Bloch wasn't supplanting me, he was practical, or he was no more than another from the charmed array that populated all the perimeters of Harry's life, but I was family. Something like that. It's pathetic, isn't it, or sad? Envy so soon after innocence. But Harry liked Bloch, for whatever reasons, his brain or plodding loyalty. And when he turned down all the senior societies, when he turned down Bones and Keys and Wolf's Head, Harry told them about Bloch. He told them about me too, and in some ways I was a more likely choice, I was on the paper, I wrote odd little occasional columns, had a story or two in the *Lit*, if I wasn't exactly clubbable at least I dressed and talked okay. But they didn't want me or Bloch. They wanted Harry.

The land coalesced dour and looming out of the dirty white vapor just as the metallic screeching on the boat bottom began. There was no moment we could have avoided it. We slid and scraped over whatever we'd hit until we came to a hard stop. By then we were listing badly. I was sure we were going to sink. Visions of *Titanic*, *Andrea Doria*, *Lusitania*, *Morro Castle*, every other ship I'd ever heard of that sank. A lot of fucks and holy fucks and holy fucking shits.

It was hard to move around in the boat, because of the list and because there were already too many of us. We crawled around the bottom as best we could inspecting for leaks and when we didn't find any Teddy shouted only semifacetiously in praise of metal boats.

We could see now that the ledge was part of a larger piece of land. "Look at this! Shit!" Teddy screamed. "We hit a whole frigging island!" We climbed out one by one onto the slippery barnacled rocks, the water lapping over our feet until we scrambled to higher ground. But Cord had an epiphany. This was Two Bush Island we had hit. It had more than two bushes on it, even the microscopic bit of it we could see, but Cord said he recognized the shape of the ledge and the rise of the land into the cloud. And from Two Bush he knew the bearing to the Bucks Harbor bell, north northwest, fifteen or seventeen degrees. So we slid on the lichen and pushed, all of us including Sascha, each with two hands on the boat like a tug-of-war, and it slipped off the rocks and we were off again, our merry little band, our beautifully screwed-up day's outing that was beautiful once again. North northwest, fifteen or seventeen degrees, we followed Cord's remembered bearing on the compass, none of us quite believing him now, because he'd hit a whole island, hadn't he? The fog was still on us, the wind was light, the outboard coughed and sputtered; we began—or perhaps was it only Bloch and myself?—to feel more like refugees than adventurers, escaping oppression somewhere or making our way from a shipwreck; but Bloch's watch didn't lie this time, and after half an hour we could hear the flat clanking of the harbor bell.

Cord let out a rebel yell signifying victory over his enemies. He steered us right for the bell. Teddy shouted he was going to hit the goddamn thing, given the talent he'd shown for hitting goddamn things. The bell got loud as a church bell. We couldn't see it till we were almost on it, and its size, tilting in the water, surprised me. It was a big red bobbing steel platform, round and about the size of a small truck if the truck was tipped up vertically. It was painted red and marked in three foot letters "BH."

The bell itself and its hammer were enclosed in bars and around the bars was a narrow perimeter, like the outer edge of a tiny carousel, where a man could stand. With each wave the bell dipped and rose, and it was this motion that caused the hammer to strike. As it loomed Harry seemed to know what he was about to do. "Hey, get in there," he yelled at Cord, "why are you such a lame southern chickenshit?"

Cord then cut the bell so close that we could touch it, and when he did that Harry crouched like a guy going to do a movie stunt, jump from a train or across buildings, and he broad-jumped at the rolling platform. By all rights he should have fallen in the water, but for a big guy he was monkey-agile, and he clung to the bars around the bell and managed to scramble and pull himself up.

He looked fierce and brave then, like a kid who had climbed a mountain. Except the mountain was dipping and rolling and Harry was holding on and the rest of us cheered and laughed in comradely fashion except Sascha, who covered her eyes. "What are you all doing?" she cried, then she saw that it was pathetic and hopeless. Cord spun the boat around the bell. Harry rained emasculating epithets on Teddy until he jumped too, but his foot slipped away and Harry had to nearly yank his arm off to save him from the bay. Now there were two of them and Cord was crazy-eager to be next, but being endlessly polite to start with and the more so the more he drank, he asked if I cared to go first. If either Bloch or I cared to go first. Well, get bent regarding that part, Cord, I certainly didn't *care* to go, I didn't say, but on the other hand it didn't look totally impossible. The others had managed it, so why couldn't I, I didn't have a limp or a heart murmur or any other IV-F excuse. Mostly I wanted to show I wasn't Bloch, who said no thanks as if he were passing up a refill of white wine, so Cord drew the skiff close again and Harry held out a bracing arm and I leapt. My ankle caught the side of the boat and I stumbled but Harry got me up there.

Cord was next. The bell dipped with the weight of all of us and now the waves of icy gray water soaked our legs. We clung to the bars and screamed like fools. I'm ashamed to say how proud I felt then. Not ashamed for what we had done, for being so appallingly young, but rather for scarcely feeling young at all, for finding youth in one fleeting moment. The others had had their fill of it, as much being young as anyone could want, and now, with Harry especially, when he did something like this it was more like a reminder, like the last times you make love to a woman. It was there but was almost gone. I felt young for once in my life.

And if I slipped and fell in the sea? If a big wave came? If we were too much weight? Then my sturdy friends, my brave friends, would save me. Or we'd all go down together and there'd be a piece in the *Times* and people would be able to see who I went down with, and somewhere there would be a plaque and maybe someone would remember. Bloch. Bloch would remember. Sascha would think we'd all been idiots, even the one she loved.

The fact was that I wasn't really afraid.

We were all fierce for a few moments. A kind of overcoming.

The bleak fog was everywhere and we could barely see ten feet.

Sascha moved the boat easily. It bobbed in and out of the fog like a quick and leery fighter. Harry was the first to have had enough or maybe he could see that Sascha was ticked. The boys had been boys long enough. Though it's a little odd, I suppose, how much we counted her one of us that afternoon. We kept saying fuck or whatever else our limited vernacular allowed. Teddy was as snide as ever. Nobody tried to be better than we were, except me, I suppose, who always did, a little bit. And Bloch.

And Sascha? She had no need to put on airs for boys. She had no airs.

She backed the stern of the skiff up to the bell, dumped it into idle and held on, as one by one we clambered back into the skiff. Bloch said he was sorry he forgot his camera. Sascha noticed that my ankle was bleeding. It was actually bleeding rather profusely, I must have scraped it on the jump but with the lashing salt water and adrenalin hadn't noticed. My friends made a fuss of it. Cord yanked a bucket of salt water from the bay to rinse it off, Harry offered a sock that he said wasn't too totally filthy though it looked otherwise, and I tied the sock around my ankle, a rough tourniquet, a kid's red badge of courage.

From the bell it was easy to feel our way around the islet and into the harbor. Finally we heard other foghorns. Lobster boats on their way to gas up. By the time we were on the mooring, the fog had lifted. Or rather, it had withdrawn. We could still see it, around the islet, south on the Reach, like some white bird of prey of extraordinary wingspan, waiting to return. Where we were, all that remained were bits of white cotton candy flying low. The sun was warm.

# CHAPTER 4

This idea I've kept, that Harry Nolan would have been or could have been or should have been. I know that objectively it's absurd. That in a country of two hundred eighty million people I should fix on one and say he was it. That he would be the hero, the redeemer, that he would win big.

And my reasons, arguably no more than snobbish and personal, crying out by association that I am or was or might have been someone too. Might have been close to someone anyway. Might have been around to tell the tale.

And the buttresses, the building blocks of my idea, these too could be ridiculed, could be found passé, prejudiced, naive; part of the problem and not the solution, isn't that what they say? Class warfare that wasn't really class warfare. For I had no class, I never did, all I had was aspiration.

Harry had drive, connections, money, wit, looks, humility and curiosity, and he was a fearless fuck. He didn't really have ideas but he knew them when he saw them.

And luck? Was he a lucky bastard too? He seemed to be.

But now let's pick him apart. Now let's see. This privilege business. Bush the current example, with his overrich Texas shtick to hide the generations of Greenwich. If people took to Bush, was it because of his privilege, or because he learned so well to hide it? And on a not-unrelated topic, how can you tell anything from someone so young, it's like picking a colt when he's six weeks old, maybe or maybe not, what will life bring, moral courage or shit, it could be any damn thing, screw the bloodlines. And going back to Yale, Harvard and Yale, aren't they the problem too, all these guys, all these leaders that often enough don't lead? Didn't they learn it all there?

Give us a man of the people, who worked summers and after school and went to Missoula State and law school at night and married his high school sweetheart and divorced. Give us a Baptist, give us a Methodist or a Catholic even; but God save us from Episcopalians and their right to rule.

And the ones who sing their praises, the ones who are so impressed, can't they see down the pike, can't they see the world for how big it is, and the need for brave hearts?

Kerry in our freshman year went around with shirts monogrammed JFK, in case anyone couldn't guess where he was headed.

Even Clinton. Even Clinton went to Yale Law. The courtship. Hillary. The TV movie crying out to be made.

So this is where the thesis of the man of the people falls down. By the 1960s the Ivy League schools were like vacuum cleaners of the nation's talent. They swooped into the smallest towns. They cleaned out whole states. All that was left when they were gone were guys who could make money. The third best thing in life. The merchant class. The grubs. The ones who didn't know there was anything but, and if late in life they were

called to do their bit, if some Republican somewhere finally re-
warded their patient contributions, they brought their blinders
with them, and their anxiety, if not their bitterness. For they
were most of them anxious by then, anxious about money and
position and some bigger boss's foot always on them, and blinded
by suspicions. Commies? Fuck 'em. Cubans? Fuck 'em. Your
black man? Fuck 'em. Cunts? Fuck 'em. Chinks fuck 'em, Frogs
fuck 'em, fucking intellectual Jews fuck 'em, Arabs fuck 'em,
gooks geeks and slopes fuck 'em. Basically, fuck 'em all.

Not that I'm taking a position here. Not that I don't see the
zircon charm in a little country club prejudice.

All I'm bearing witness to is that sometime postwar our nation culled a leadership class and concentrated it in a few schools.
If you didn't get in, you probably had to work for a living. If you
got in you might still have to work, but maybe not. You might get
to teach. You might get to see your spirit soar. You might turn
into a preposterous old queen. You might write, take drugs, eat
shit and die. Or you might, if ten other things turned out right,
get to lead.

So let's narrow the field. It wasn't Harry against two hundred
million. It was Harry against, say, several thousand. Many of whom
were rich and driven, a few of whom were fearless, some of whom
were connected, witty, curious, humble, good-looking, and/or
lucky. And how many were all of these? I don't really know.

\*

Harry's plan for getting there. One. Enlist in the military.
Two. Go to law school at Stanford or Boalt Hall. Three. Do public

policy law a couple of years and run for Congress in a decently safe Bay Area district (one or another was always coming along). Four. Serve in the House until his father retired from the Senate. Five. Do *not* immediately run for his father's seat because that would smack of nepotism and maybe turn people away, *but* . . . Six. Run for the other Senate seat the next year it came available, by which time the nostalgia for Nolan, the memories of the white fox, would be burning bright and Harry would be the obvious beneficiary. Seven. On from there.

This was not a plan Harry came up with himself. One of Senator Nolan's advisors proposed it to him on a Christmas ski vacation in Mammoth. But Harry was quite proud of it, in a cynical, joshing way. "Hey Louie, I've got a plan. Kerry's got a plan, so I've got a plan."

He laid it out for me in Yorky Yorkside's coffee shop on York in low conspiratorial tones.

"I want to know what position I might hope for in a future Nolan administration," I said.

"What do you have in mind, son?"

"Court Jew?"

But overall, none of it was a joke.

*

The origins of the meritocracy:

One. In the Depression, and its legacy that the rich were to blame, and that smart people in government could bring us out of it.

Two. In the War, and the rising democratic expectations of those who fought and won it.

Three. In the Cold War, and Sputnik, and the felt need that we would have to harness every bit of the nation's native talent in order to defeat the insidious enemy.

Four. In the College Board exams, that gave the elite colleges a way to pick the most promising from the most obscure high schools across the country.

Five. In the goodwill of people like Inslee Clark, Yale's admissions director who wore his pink-cheeked white shoe preppiness like camouflage, who made it his calling to bring Yale into the new democratic age.

Six. In the traditional ruling class fear, particularly strong in the United States where so many rough-edged guys got the ruling class going, that if they didn't get some new blood in there soon the whole thing would go to pot.

Seven. In the Holocaust, though it wasn't called that then, but anyway a slight softening of the contours of traditional anti-Semitism, in the guilty aftermath of catastrophe.

# CHAPTER 5

*For thousands of days Shiva was united with Parvati,*
*and that contact transmitted a tremor to the earth.*
—Roberto Calasso

Stasis. Hanging out. The dance of nothingness. Afternoon.

We were back at the house by three o'clock. At the Bucks Harbor Marine they were saying there were still mackerel around. They weren't running exactly, but they were around, and the "around" made them sound like a legend, a vague presence, a school of ghosts. Cord wanted to go get some and he dug poles with rusted mackerel jigs on them out of a cobwebbed corner of the shed. The day was mellow now. The sun came and went but the mosquitoes mostly stayed. Cord took Teddy and Bloch with him. There were some rocks to the south of the cove and that's where they were going. I stayed behind. Harry and Sascha went into their room and closed the door.

I re-bandaged my ankle with gauze and then I read awhile, feeling proprietary, in an armchair downstairs. Some years-old magazine about Life in Maine, with twelve tips on what to do with a pumpkin and getting your gun ready for hunting season. And L. L. Bean ads in black and white. They had fewer items then; boots, waders, chamois shirts. Remember the *Whole Earth Catalog*? This was before the *Whole Earth Catalog*. The big room downstairs faced the water, but the windows looking onto it were narrow and wouldn't open. I guessed it was to keep the winter out, no compromise with the howling winter, every little bit helps. On the mantel were carved boats signed "P. Elliott, 1934," and there were two lamps made out of liquor bottles on a desk that had birch logs for legs. I was beginning to feel at home in my genteel snooping around. In a corner on a table I found a photo of a girl I knew to be Cord's sister, in the sash and crown of a beauty queen, kissing Elvis Presley on the cheek. He wasn't kissing her, she was kissing him. She must have been standing on a step or a platform because he was looking slightly up at her. She was Miss Memphis County Fair or something similar and he was so young he wasn't famous yet, bright eyes and cheeks and the trace of a smirk, playing the county fair, and Cord's sister was making his day.

At first I wasn't aware what went on upstairs. It started like occasional gunfire, a voice raised here or there. "Your father." "Shut up!" "Always your father!" They must have been moving around, a door opened, and for a little while I heard more. "This is crazy. Would you fucking calm down?" "Don't talk to me! Just go away!" "I'm going! I'm going soon enough!" "Go rattle your sabers with somebody else, I don't care!" Their voices parched in a way that I didn't know them. I gave up any pretense of going about my business, which is to say my downstairs poking around, and strained my ears toward the stairs. Another lull. A door. Harry pacing in the upstairs corridor, into the bathroom, out of the bathroom. "You knew what I was doing all along!" "I didn't know you'd be this *stu*pid about it!" "You're the one that's stupid!" My heart being bounced like a ball. "You idiot! I'm afraid!" "Oh, the sympathy vote!" "Fuck you." "Fuck yourself." These being some of the things that were said by the ones I loved, who sounded mortal enough then.

If Harry and Sascha had a fight. If Shiva and Parvati had a fight. The real fight would be in silence. He said, she said, so on. These are the things great lovers say their fights are about, or that people like me overhear and report and analyze, but really the fight has no words, as the deep of the ocean has no words. Or anyway it was something close to this I told myself and half-believed, as Harry tramped down the stairs past me, muttering "Hey Louie" softly, his eyes rimmed with red.

He pushed the screen door open with his foot and went outside. I waited what I imagined was a respectful moment, a moment that would suggest no urgent curiosity on my part, then went out to see. He had the hood of the Aston Martin up and was tinkering underneath it with a wrench and a screwdriver and a dirty rag that he laid on the fender to protect the paint job the way mechanics do. I approached him and he said "Hey Louie" again, as if he'd forgotten he'd just said it, in a flat tone, and he didn't look up.

It seemed more manly to me not to have overheard them, and not to admit it even if I had. Though how could Harry have thought I had not? Or was I only learning a first lesson in weekend houseguest politesse?

"What are you doing?" I asked. Cleaning the plugs, setting the timing, something like that. Harry was always doing something to his Aston Martin, so it made as convenient an excuse for him as for me. It was a pretty bad car. You hear Aston Martin, you think hundreds of thousands of dollars or even back then tens of thousands. But I never thought it cost that much. He'd bought it in Paris off a guy he met at American Express and had it shipped back. It often didn't run, which Teddy explained by the fact that Harry worked on it. Harry was always threatening never to give Teddy a ride in it again. But he liked to give people rides. In fact he liked to lend his car out. Which maybe was why it was always broken. He asked me why I hadn't gone fishing with the others.

I shrugged. My ankle, and anyway I didn't feel like it.

Then he told a mackerel joke, which of course was also a pussy joke, though I don't remember it now. And about the flesh of mackerel, he was onto mackerel now, it wasn't always salty and gamy, not if you cooked it fast, he said, if you cooked it an hour after you caught it, the flesh was sweet and delicious.

I said fuck the mackerel, we were getting lobsters later. The rims of his eyes were still swollen with anger but I didn't say anything about it.

All this time he didn't look up. He grabbed his screwdriver and did something jagged with it and cursed.

If Harry and Sascha had a fight. If Shiva and Parvati had a fight. There would be a moment when she would appear less magnificent to him. For a moment in his anger he would fuck a cow if it was around. But she would see this and scorn him on account of it, and in her scorn he would see her magnificence return, and be overcome with remorse and desire.

"Louie, you know what, buddy? I *am* a hypocrite."

"What?"

He started changing the oil. Something else to do.

"And you know what else? You were right."

"About what?"

"What you said."

"What did I say?"

"To Sascha. When you're doing your duty as opposed to doing it so other people will think so. I can see that," he said.

And I thought what a simple pure mind his was and what a patronizing shit I was in ways, unlike Harry, that I didn't know how to say.

"I don't know," I said.

"You don't have to get yourself shot at. That's not what I'm saying. I'm talking about me, what a pompous jerk I am."

If Harry and Sascha had a fight. If Shiva and Parvati had a fight. They would have to work it out. He with no choice but to start over. The grin. The wit. The gesture. The capacity to bet it all, to say fuck you not to her but to the universe; or to give that impression, to let her think that, to be a little sly. While she's not sure. She's charmed but wary. Her memory warns her but it's growing dim. The scene goes on, as structured as a ritual dance.

Harry's under the car now, unscrewing the oil plug, his hairy legs sticking out. I'm still hanging around. The conversation reaches a dead end. How can I talk about getting a deferment when he's going to the war in a week? And Sascha told him everything I said and he wasn't even pissed. He's praising me! What the fuck for? So now we're talking about Ft. Ord, which is where he will be going. It's in California somewhere, of course, but I don't have a clear geographic fix on it. Harry really loves California. He talks about climbing in the Sierras. From Ft. Ord, if he has weekend leave, he'll get back up there, he'll drive all night, he'll hike around. Now he comes out from under the car pulling the pan with the dirty oil after him. It can't be a very good car because he changes the oil often and it's sludgy black in the pan. He complains about this. The engine's a piece of shit and will have to be rebuilt, he says.

The bottoms of his eyes are still red and all the while that we talk about the car and the guy in Los Gatos who rebuilds sports car engines and Ft. Ord and the future and never once mention Vietnam, I'm ashamed because some part of me is starting to act up again, the part that was never content with the peace I made, the rebel part, like some guys in the hills wondering what the news from the city really meant. That is to say, their fighting again. That is to say, Harry going away. Judas thoughts or brave thoughts, depending whose life you believed in, whose was the main narrative line. Rebels dream about cracks in the kingdom. They wait and have no pity for those they love.

Not that the rebel was strong in me. I felt faint stirrings, not much more. Mostly I was a loyal subject. A flag waver, a guy you could count on, a bit player who knows his part.

But it made me a little slow with Harry, as though I was thinking twice. And who was the innocent one here, I with my rare love for him or he who didn't seem to recognize all my pathetic contradictions? Maybe both of us were. He started putting his tools away. His hands were black with grease and there were smudge marks on his face. The kitchen screen door scraped and banged. God how loud it sounded then, as if it were the only sound on earth. Harry looked her way, got nothing back. I also looked, feeling a tightness, gray fear, in my neck.

She walked in our direction with no more expression than a sock doll. Two eyes a nose a slightly downturned mouth, and dark restless hair, as if there was Jewish blood in there somewhere, though if there was, none of us knew where. Did I tell you she was going to medical school? In January she was starting science courses so that she could get into med school the year following. It's I suppose why I'd been surprised to see her with a summer novel. She'd brought a biology book up with her, as thick as the Boston phone book. Though again, she was an omnivorous reader, one of those pre-Raphaelite beauties, otherwise restless, who would sit still for books, Gide, Proust, Pushkin, Italian novelists, Germans.

Harry looked her way again and his eyes asked, What the fuck?

What the fuck nothing you fuck. Don't you know the word nothing? Nothing is nothing. You don't exist.

She walked to the car. There was something she wanted to get out of it.

Harry went back to his screwdriver and wrench. All his little instruments, lined up in a row, as though they would offer some kind of protection, some recourse, in case this turned out badly.

She got her biology book off the floor on the passenger side. What it was doing there I didn't know, since it had been downstairs in the morning. Or maybe it was a two-volume set.

He whispered through his teeth, as she slammed the door, "You asshole." By which I guess he meant you wouldn't be out here if you didn't love me, admit it, you skinny bitch.

He caught her in a sidelong glance and she turned and whacked his head with the book.

She got in a pretty fair shot, almost a cartoon shot, the flat of the cover as if making an exclamatory THWACK! right on the side of his crewcut.

I knew it was over then. I knew they'd be in bed in an hour and they were.

The rebels who dreamed of an independent me, a day when King Louie would seize the throne, retreated to their mountain caves where they belonged.

It was past six o'clock and if you were upstairs you could hear Parvati's tender defeated moans, when the fishermen came home from the sea. None of them had caught anything but Bloch, who had two skinny mackerel on a string.

# CHAPTER 6

Where am I now? Far away from all of this. Most of a continent away. Much of a lifetime away.

Have I learned anything at all in the meantime? Of course. The cost of living and the scores of games and more names for things than there really are things. The limits of irony. The limits of very nearly everything except love, and maybe the limits of love too.

Interior exterior I've written a lot of scenes. How many of them do I still believe in? Or really, did I ever believe in?

And yet I seem to believe in these, the scenes of my youth, improbable, naive. I believe in their beauty, oddly enough, at a time when beauty is derided, denied, relegated by right-thinking people to the kitsch dreams of simpletons and fools. Beauty is not trusted, and I suppose that's right. Beauty can never be trusted, which is part of why it's beautiful. And nobility, the evil twin's twin? We don't carry that stuff anymore. Maybe we could special-order it.

I was scarcely a man in 1966. Did I tell you my father had gone away? My father had gone away long before and I suppose that I was looking for him. And then Harry Nolan came along.

Sons of disappeared fathers, unite. There are still men out there to believe in, or if you're too wounded, to betray.

Not that any of that matters. Time passes, and none of our fathers are good enough, and then they're all we have.

\*

Things that were never so about Harry and Sascha in relation to me.

That I ever told her that I loved her.

That either of them knew. Or if they knew, they didn't care, not too much anyway, because people were supposed to love them. They didn't go out of their way to seek it but it was kind of inevitable, the same as trust funds were inevitable or someone to write a letter for them, someone who knew someone, no matter what it was they wanted or where they were going; and if they thought about it too much every time it happened, it could throw them off, make them a little crazy.

They'd known each other three years. During that time they'd been back and forth between Cambridge and New Haven. Sascha often stayed in our rooms, but Yale still had rules with the archaic-poetic name, parietals, which boiled down meant no girls overnight, so they had to be sort-of careful. A couple of times they broke up. When she wasn't around, Harry was an aficionado of townies and streetmeat. He could be walking back from the library and arrive with four girls at our place. He was always getting laid, he got laid more than anyone I knew. Most of us didn't get laid at all. But none of it meant anything when it came to her. He could rest his head on any part of her and read a book and be content. He worshiped her. He did what she said.

Flashback interior exterior series of shots New York day night June. The wedding, the events leading up to it.

A cattle call for aristocrats. Ambassadors to here and there (Sascha's father had been ambassador to Italy), foundation types (Sascha's father had also been head of the Carnegie Endowment), bankers from Chase, investment bankers from Brown Brothers, lawyers from Debevoise, doctors from Columbia P & S (Sascha's uncle was head of cardiac surgery), cold warrior types, philanthropists, women who painted or had galleries or gardened, a few dames and drones and polo players and people who were plain rich.

And that's not yet counting the California contingent, the Nolans and St. Christophers, who were this and that in San Francisco, who were said to run the opera there and anything else they cared to run, and the senator himself, the white fox of the west.

Though if I could highlight any one it would be Sascha's Uncle Timothy, who wore a bowtie and covered his forehead with a sweep of thin silky hair. Uncle Timothy was an old white-shoe CIA guy who thought up the plan of dropping extra-extra-large condoms on the Soviet Union, all of them marked "Made in USA," to demoralize the enemy. Why highlight him? No good reason, really, I just thought he was funny, like an older version of Teddy, I could see Teddy in the CIA, thinking up psy-ops, dropping the condoms, having a laugh. Maybe if it had been farther back in time. By our time the Cold War was pretty humorless, the Cuban missile crisis, Sputnik, Vietnam.

At the rehearsal dinner I made a toast. All the ushers had to. Mine was flat and labored, about how the Nolans and the Maclarens had been secretly and fatefully mis-meeting for two or three hundred years. I'd been working on it for days, until it had come to seem like one of those little square plastic puzzles where you try to get the numbers in order but two always wind up inverted. 1 2 3 4 5 6 7 8 9 10 11 12 14 13 15.

Or I thought it was lame anyway, but it got a few laughs, and afterward Sascha's mother came up to me and told me what a hoot it had been. She used that word, "hoot," that sounded so much like the forties. She had a big smile, bigger than Sascha's, especially for the size of her mouth, as though she could devour you if she wanted to, and her face was strong-boned and lined and a little bit tragic. She said my toast was the best of the night and asked if she could have a copy. From this I concluded for a minute or two that the Establishment welcomed me with open arms.

Then at the Yale Club where they were putting up the out-of-town ushers, in my sliver of a room on an airshaft, I dreamed that Sascha was in the room with me, in the narrow bed. She had her clothes on and I had on mine as though we'd just kind of fallen into this, suddenly and without preparation, but our legs were intertwined and her face was close to mine, bigger than I'd ever seen it in my life, and her smile was like her mother's smile. She touched the side of my face. She held my face. Her hand was cool. I kissed it. We kissed. Her face was so close it was like I was seeing it for once in my life, little marks, blemishes, rivulets, rises and falls, little lines on her lips, her dark hair, her dark eyes like blue coals. Her tongue, I tasted her tongue, and she smiled her mother's smile so sweetly and voraciously that I knew we'd reached an understanding of a lifetime and that it was a dream.

How could it not be a dream if Harry wasn't even mentioned? And then of course he was mentioned, in the not-mentioning of him he was there, somewhere, in the dream, hovering, telling me how right this was, he concurred a hundred percent, life had a way of coming out fairly. I woke up in a sweetness of my whole body so intense and enveloping that if I'd had an orgasm just then it would scarcely have registered. I tried to go back to the dream, refuting pale, aching reality on the grounds that the other had all the truth of my life. But there was light in the airshaft somewhere and the sweetness drained away.

There are dreams that are prophecies and there are dreams that are as close as it gets.

The wedding went off without any fool like me standing up with hoarsely voiced objections. At four in the afternoon of the nineteenth of June in Riverside Church, up by Columbia, presided over by the Reverend William Sloan Coffin, Yale's chaplain who'd been arrested in Mississippi and was the champion of so many liberal causes that the FBI would eventually put him up there with Dr. Spock among the country's top-ranked delusional misguided corrupters of youth. A lot of DKE guys showed up for the wedding, though I don't remember Bush as one of them and I doubt he was invited. The prettiest bridesmaid was Sascha's sister Maisie, who'd just turned nineteen and had astonishing red hair and Sascha's lank build and in her close orbit an "admirer," as her parents might have put it, a beautiful slender black-haired kid from Venice who was bumming around the New York art world for a year. Harry looked like a shark with gleaming teeth in his wedding suit and Sascha's skin had never looked so pale. They did it all with ironic smiles and easy grace, as though they'd already long been married. There were so many people there who seemed to have known one another forever, cousins who'd grown up together in summer places, bridesmaids who'd gone out with Cord's or Teddy's prep school roommates, people who'd all been to the same deb parties in New York or Philadelphia. I seated a lot of WASPs.

How do you feel when you lose? Some baseball wise guy must have answered that one. You feel like a loser.

Or in my case you follow the lead of Teddy Redmond for a little while, trying to charm one or another of the bridesmaids into a drunken encounter in a closet, and failing that, when none of them even bothers to smile back at you, sensing, perhaps, your halfheartedness or the mark of the interloper in your brown eyes and uncertain carriage, you dance once with the bride, finding her face close to yours in a way utterly unlike your dream. Sascha was radiant with goodwill that day. Either that or she was great at putting it on. "Louie, are you having a *great* time?" "Louie, I'm going to introduce you to some *girls*." I stepped on her toes once and she wasn't wearing shoes and when she laughed it off I wondered if I would ever know one single thing she felt. Then, getting back to the second person, you say congrats to the groom, hug him because he hugged you first, sense his openheartedness and graciousness and decide he's a thousand times better than you, and say good-bye before the cake is cut, pleading indigestion.

The Maclarens supplied a car to ferry people back to midtown so I didn't have to take the bus in my tails. At the Yale Club I changed into my street clothes and then wandered over to Eighth Avenue. Exterior interior New York night junkies and whores. I found a girl who looked at me back and for fifteen dollars she took me to a room on Forty-eighth Street and sucked me off. I assumed she was a junkie but she didn't seem to mind what she was doing and her lips were supple and sweet and enough like Sascha's in my dream that for a few moments I was happy. When we were done a friend of the girl's came in. She was a bigger girl and I didn't know what she was doing there but she said did I know that the girl wasn't really a girl. The girl, my girl, said don't listen to the other one, she's crazy, and we left.

# CHAPTER 7

The sun moved toward evening. I never used to notice where the sun was in the sky but I noticed it then, like a slowly ticking clock. Which brings to mind that a clock is made in the sun's image and not the other way around, but a city kid has to start somewhere. You could see for miles to the southeast from Clements Cove, over the low huddled islands and the Reach and the southern bay. I checked a chart on the wall downstairs. I wanted to make what I saw official. The cabins and the dock and woods across the cove took on a gilded clarity, as though a Venetian painter had lit them up. An eagle flapped its wings in the topknot of a spruce. The flank of an open boat spread out its wavering crimson shadow on the water. Venetian light. Out there somewhere was the fog, but I couldn't see it.

We got lobsters from the Bucks Harbor Marine and dumped them in a black kettle that covered all the burners on the stove and ate them sitting on driftwood on the pebbled beach. The mosquitoes dined on us. We passed around 6-12, because Cutters hadn't been invented yet or hadn't reached Maine, but it was oily and only half-worked. Teddy in particular kept slapping away at the air or his own flesh with righteous vengeance. "Beast of the ocean! Get out of my tomalley, you beast!"

"They like that aftershave you're wearing," Cord opined.

"Fuck you, I don't wear aftershave."

"You don't wear that Skin Bracer shit? I thought you were a Mennen Skin Bracer man."

"Screw you. Jesus, these bugs!"

"Brought 'em up from the swamp in Tennessee."

"*That* I believe. Isn't that your family business? Aren't you all bug farmers?"

"They like soft Greenwich boys."

"Jesus!" Swatting at the air.

"See they don't bite Louie. New Yorkers are too tough for 'em. Too tough and mean."

My facetious rueful smile.

Harry and Sascha were becalmed now. J.b.f., just been fucked, is what used to be said and maybe still is. And I was becalmed. The approach to evening. The cold, clear country, as though the sweat of the world had been wiped from it. These friends, like figures of this landscape, who drove me up and gave everybody shit and didn't seem to mind me. And Harry and Sascha like restored monarchs, the king and queen are *back,* folks, let's give 'em a big hand! That is, together, tolerant, slightly sardonic, quiet. And easy at heart, whatever that means. Or maybe what it meant was that when Sascha's troubled heart rested in his, it truly rested. Sascha on a rock with her lobster, knees together maneuvering with a pair of pliers and one of those sterling silver pokers. She had a surgeon's way about her, deliberate and patient. Even when she cracked a claw she hardly made a sound.

What was this "troubled heart" business? What was her heart troubled about? I never really knew, and it's possible Harry didn't either, he only knew what he could do about it. Or not to be mysterious: Sascha may have been a little bored by life. By much of it anyway. She had trouble finding its primary colors. Where this started, though, and what could explain it, the determination of a cause—I don't really trust causes. Not concerning those I've loved, anyway. Causes distract from what is. And you never hear the end of them, there's always one more, and meanwhile the one you love could choke on a bone or go blind.

Sometimes people try too hard to say something, the world becomes clotted in their minds and takes on unreal shapes. We were quiet so long that Bloch must have thought it was his fault we were quiet, or his obligation as the witty, intelligent, serious guest to do something about it. Am I being too rough with Bloch? Am I importing what I felt then into what I feel now? Sometimes like a CD in skip mode I tell this story and the years collapse, as if they never were.

A fault, an error, or simply a fate?

What gives me the strength to go back, I suppose, is that I've never entirely left, like one who still wears the clothes, the styles, of his youth, who parts his hair as hair was parted then. Which by the way I think is a not-ungallant thing, loyal in a way, a not-unmanly thing.

Bloch asked Harry if he knew where he was going to be sent. He was a little earnest when he said it, not enough to be cloying, but enough to let everybody know that he'd been mulling what had been said before, that he was sincere and concerned about it.

Harry said Ft. Ord but Bloch said he meant after basic, did Harry know where he was going after that.

Harry said he didn't know.

Bloch could have shut up then. He could tell from our faces, mine and Cord's anyway, which were set in a way to endure discomfort, that we wanted him to, that enough was enough, that we'd gone this way already and what was the point. I felt again as though the conversation was headed where I had no right to be, where I'd already trespassed once and gotten away with it. But Bloch plowed on, saying he'd heard, he'd read, it wasn't necessarily Vietnam you got sent to, only a certain percentage got sent to Vietnam, it could be Germany, he said.

"Maybe," Harry said.

"Maybe they'll send you to Heidelberg and you can duel," Teddy said.

"That's stupid," Cord said.

But we couldn't get off it now, we went around in circles as if some experimental scientist in a funny hat had hypnotized us, until Sascha said, "He's going to Vietnam. Of course he is."

"What about being a cameraman?" I asked, and when Harry only shrugged I went on, as if I was bundling the conversation into the back seat of a car to drive it out of town, about how they'd probably have him filling sandbags for a year.

"That's what Calvert did," Cord said, and enough of us nodded sagely.

But Bloch seemed still to want to get to the bottom of something.

"It's a colonial war," he said. "They shouldn't have a draft for a colonial war."

"I volunteered," Harry said.

"But would you have if there wasn't a draft?"

Harry paused and sucked on his lobster shell. "Maybe," he said.

"But if there was no draft, even if you were going into politics, you wouldn't have to. It's the draft that makes it necessary."

"So fucking what?" Teddy said.

"So, are you going? Are any of us, but him?" Bloch must have known he'd said more than he wanted to. He didn't want to be hated, after all. He wanted to be liked, for his acuity, his sensitivity to undercurrent, and in the end, his reasoned sympathy. Whereas I thought, just then, how brilliant do you have to be to say there's a gorilla in the house when everyone already smells it. "I mean, that's not the point anyway," Bloch said. "I just think it's going to come out badly, having a draft to fight a colonial war."

Which finally got out of Teddy, "What's this colonial war shit? We're fighting communism, for chrissake."

But Bloch had had enough. His dark eyes had a dull hurt in them, as if he'd come up once again against the inevitable obstacle, the monolithic sheer stupidity, that had somehow continued to confront him, the honest broker of blunt reason, at every turn of his life.

"I'm sorry I brought it up," Bloch said.

Are you really, I thought, you self-pitying passive-aggressive piece of shit. The truth was that the better Bloch's points were, the more I feared him then. I wanted to make a better point than he did, I wanted to make a point that would shut him up. A showdown of the intellectuals, of the meritocrats, only one comes out alive. But Bloch had already shut himself up.

And wasn't it also true of Bloch that he used ideas to advance himself and not the ideas themselves? As had I twice already today, with Sascha on the island, with Harry at the car. Couldn't I be cursed by association? Better, like a liberal after the war issuing an anticommunist denunciation, to draw the bright line between us, his side, my side, my side being our side, our little band whatever it stood for.

But as I say, Bloch had already shut himself up, so what could I say?

"Aren't you going to finish those feelers, Adam?" Harry said, and when Bloch shook his head, Harry sucked them clean.

We washed our hands in the salt water that lapped on the pebbles by our feet and Cord brought down one of the bags the lobsters came in and we dumped our carcasses in it.

When he brought the bag he also brought a football. No white stripes, no NFL endorsements. From the lacing it looked prewar. Cord could throw a football easily and with accuracy thirty yards and sometimes thirty-five. He was Yale's third-string quarterback our sophomore year but the guys ahead of him were better and he saw no way up and he took an interest about the same time in a girl at Sweetbriar, which was a hard weekend trip, and a smaller interest in the English metaphysical poets, and so he quit. His name wasn't going to be added to the Elliotts of Yale athletic fame but he was still a pretty fair athlete, and when it came to touch football he was competitive as hell.

He must have brought out the football as a way of changing the subject, the way the hostess of a dinner party would if a guest started talking about new foods that cause cancer. He didn't ask if anybody wanted to play, he just chose up sides.

We played on the beach. A fall meant cuts from the mussel shells, but no one fell. Basically it was Harry against Cord, Cord who loved to beat Harry and Harry who hated to lose to Cord, who he referred to as the winged wonder.

The rest of us were bit players, though I could run a little bit and my hands were not bad and Teddy was a swirl of gangly moves.

We were losing the sun. It got hard to see the ball. But the game seemed to loosen us up. It wasn't that we wanted to forget that Harry was going away, it was more that we couldn't forget. Talking about it just seemed to make lies of it. Witness just before, and don't even mention Bloch, just observe the generic principle. You're going to say something to make things better, to put it all in perspective, to make a joke of it, but what you say actually is something to make you look good, make you look like the sage or the wit or the compassionate one, the number-one guy. Well screw you bullshit shut up and leave it alone. It wasn't a joke and we couldn't make it better, or that's what we thought anyway. Or it's what I thought "we" thought, drawing the circle again close to my heart. We couldn't make it better, so we played touch football instead.

I caught one of the winged wonder's bombs and our side went up a touchdown as the sun got fat and squat in the western sky behind us. We were playing until it was gone. You couldn't tell with Harry sometimes whether he was angry or facetious, he was a deadpan kind of guy, his jokes were always flat and smileless and you had to figure out if the punchline had come yet because he never let you know, but (as I said) he hated to lose to Cord, mostly because of Cord's unbearable crowing when he won. So Harry marched his little squad back down the beach, two-minute drill precision, short passes to Teddy, three complete and a first. Sascha was our pass rusher who chased Harry around like a fool, both of them laughing, Harry feinting and dodging. He always got his pass off and afterward she always pushed him.

Our goal being the invisible line between Cord's sweatshirt and my sweater. As they got closer there was less room for Teddy to run and we held them better. Finally it was fourth down and they needed a completion for a first and only a spreading pencil-line of pink still showed in the west. Cord was yelling "Sundown! Sundown!" It was making Harry crazy. They broke their huddle and did a three-man team's version of lining up. Bloch hiked, but instead of putting his arms together to block he ducked back and took a handoff from Harry, who darted away from Sascha and was open by five yards in the end zone. Teddy had gone deep and Cord though long-limbed and quick couldn't cover both. We didn't even think Bloch could pass a football. But of course anybody can, a little bit at least, and all he had to do was lob it anywhere in Harry's direction. I started toward Harry. I was going to be way too late but then I saw Bloch hesitating, his eyes darting between Harry and the hole I'd left behind. Harry yelled for the ball and waved his arms like a guy on a desert island at the first passing ship in years but Bloch decided to run. It was only those few yards, after all. He wasn't that slow and he ran easily around Sascha, to the left, toward the goal line where I had been. I darted back and nailed him with two hands front and back while he was still a couple of feet short. Feeling vengeance on all fronts, his sweaty solidity, his hard breath, feeling like I'd nabbed one of the Beagle Boys—and getting ready for my picture in the *Duckburg Gazette*?

Bloch looked surprised, as though to ask where the hell I'd come from, I who was going the other way the last time he'd looked. Cord whooped like the Grays had won the war. Sascha didn't know what had happened except the sun was down and the game was over and she was glad of it. Harry glowered. He said to Bloch, "I was wide open, Adam."

"Sorry," Bloch said.

"The play was, you pass."

"I saw this hole. Sorry."

"What hole? Shit."

"I thought. I don't know. I don't know what I was thinking," Bloch said. "Sorry."

He'd been afraid to throw a bad pass, which made running look like a better bet. We all knew it, but he couldn't say it, it was like a stone in his throat.

Harry yelled at Cord, "Hey, winged wonder—you're a lucky fuck!" He seemed annoyed only at Bloch, and a guilty pleasure grazed me, as though I was nine years old and had gotten a kid who had it coming in trouble.

We all went inside. Bloch held his head high and didn't say anything, but his neck looked stiff.

# CHAPTER 8

Scenes I never saw. The legendary, sort of, Harry Nolan.

*Harry in Mississippi, in the middle of the fall term, in October of 1963, in a room in the jailhouse in Hattiesburg, telling Allard Lowenstein off.*

Lowenstein being the guy who'd got him down there in the first place. Al is in the history books now, a small white figure in glasses somewhere at the back of the civil rights movement, and maybe there's even been a movie about him because years later one of his disciples shot him dead. He came to Yale in the fall of sixty-three, one of those early Pied Piper activists of the sixties, recruiting volunteers for a cause of his own invention, a "Freedom Vote" in Mississippi. Harry heard him speak in the Political Union and went out for coffee with him after. What was said about Lowenstein at the time made him seem like an adult version of Adam Bloch. That is, in the parlance and character analysis of the era, he was either a weenie, a flamer, a tubesteak, or all three. But according to Harry he was kind of a fearless bastard.

And this thing he'd thought up, the Freedom Vote, was clever and brave in a way that things seldom manage to be at the same time. The Negroes, who weren't being allowed to register, would get to vote in a mock election instead. It was to be an exercise in confidence-building, in consciousness-raising, and publicity, and the role of the white students from the north was to solicit the Negroes to vote in it and simply by being there to draw the nation's attention to the effort.

The setting and the sentences are lost to me, but when Harry came from talking to Allard Lowenstein he used the word "justice." I remember it for how odd it sounded, that word with its granite finality being applied to something in our everyday lives, rather than as a concept out of Plato or some other thin paperback. Probably he used the word several times. Justice. Justice. Justice. A word that even today when I hear it as the last name of someone, the ballplayer Dave Justice or a guy I knew from law school, Bob Justice, who wound up a judge in Indiana, Justice Justice, seems out of proportion, dramatic, solitary. The scales. The blindfold. The bearer of vast hopes.

The civil rights workers, the three from the north, hadn't been murdered yet.

Harry decided he was going to Mississippi. Cord had a southerner's sort of objection. In the end he thought it wasn't courteous. Harry said oh no, it was going to be incredibly courteous, people were going to be sitting around drinking mint juleps with each other, it was going to be unbelievably fucking courteous. Fuck you, Cord said with impeccable courtesy, northern piece of shit troublemaker, but if Harry was stopping in Memphis he could stay with Cord's family.

One thing more I remember: the incongruity, the leap, of it being Harry who was going down there. He was pledging DKE.

He was a quasi-jock, not some wonk from Bronx Science. He was a Democrat because his father was a Democrat, but his father wasn't a raging leftie, he was the sort of Democrat who was a confidant of JFK and a good pal of Douglas Aircraft, of old Don Douglas himself. It was said there'd never been a defense bill Senator Hal Nolan disliked. Harry wasn't standing in his father's tradition to go to Mississippi, he was running way ahead of it, he was staking out fresh ground.

But he went, while the rest of us wrote papers about this and that and dreamed lurid dreams of Dartmouth weekend.

In his laconic, Gary Cooper version of it, Harry had a run-of-the-mill time there. He walked the auburn dirt roads and knocked on the tin and paper shacks like a tourist of misery, and passed out dummy ballots and tried to get the sharecroppers who were often scared out of their drawers to listen to or even look at him. He was called a nigger-lover in various tones of voice, had a shotgun waved in his direction by a skinny shit in a truck, tried unsuccessfully to charm the Hattiesburg police, got arrested and dumped in jail.

But the scene I care to remember, I can't precisely, because when he came back he only alluded to it. It's the one that could have happened to Harry Nolan alone, and it doesn't make him a hero, it only gives a glimpse of where for a moment he was.

He's in the Hattiesburg drunk tank and it's not really too bad with eight people in it. The food's pathetic and you piss in tin cans but there's camaraderie and a dumb pride and less fear than on the open roads where you were never sure about the next pickup truck. Lowenstein shows up. After a peptalk to all, he wants to speak with Harry. He persuades the chief of police to give them a room, which isn't so hard since the chief looks forward to listening in.

Allard says to Harry, "Have you told your father?"

Harry says to Allard, "What, that I'm down here? I've told him. He doesn't know I'm in jail, I don't think."

Allard says to Harry, "See but this is it, this is our good shot."

"What's our good shot?" Harry asks.

"'Senator Nolan's son arrested.' That's news. That's drama. What's the senator going to do?"

"You let that out, you lean on that, Al, and you're dead."

"Excuse me?"

"You won't use my father like that. You won't use me against my father like that. Try it and I'll tell every reporter in the county about this conversation. And I'll have Chief Lardass outside the door to confirm it, Al."

So maybe the dialogue's compressed and a tad on the snappy side but something like that was said. I knew it because he told us he went down there on condition he be treated like everyone else and his father not be involved. I knew it further because it's what Harry alluded to, that Lowenstein approached him with a publicity angle. And the story never came out. No one even reported that Senator Nolan's son was down there.

*Harry in Millbrook, N.Y., at the Hitchcock estate, dropping acid with Leary and Alpert.*

This was in the spring of sixty-four and it's possible the phrase "dropping acid" hadn't been invented yet. Leary and Alpert had been booted out of Harvard on account of their experiments but some rich kid had given them his house in Dutchess County to carry on. Harry was taking a psychology course in fear and courage from a guy named Webber, and this Webber was a proto-hipster who grew outsized sideburns for the time and flew a plane.

J. Lewis

Webber was a pal of Leary and Alpert's and made weekend flights to Millbrook. He invited his students to come along. He made it seem that if you were the kind of person to be taking a course in fear and courage in the first place, this was a thing you wouldn't want to miss.

Most of Webber's students declined for no better reason than that they secretly didn't want to be flying on any plane that he was piloting. Very reasonable, thought Harry, but he went anyway. It's been written in books what happened those weekends in Millbrook, but it's been so many years since I read any of them that I've forgotten. Who was fucking who if anybody, whether there were experiments that felt like science or just everybody getting high. I don't have a bibliography. But I do know the phrase "bad trip" had been invented by then, because Harry talked about a poor guy who'd had one and embraced a cow the way Nietzsche embraced a horse when he had gone crazy from syphilis. Harry did not. He saw colors and stars and galaxies and flew around and he told us he ran into Sascha in deep space. We thought he might be going insane. Our blessed bourgeois perspective, which I still sort of love and have hardly the will to escape. But Harry wasn't going insane, he was just having little epiphanies that we were not, seeing the world inside out, and having some fun while he was at it. As best I can remember he spared us the word "profound." But he wanted me in particular to come, "Hey Louie—it's right in your strike zone, it's philosophical," he thought it would loosen me up and do me some good, and when I passed he called me a pussy. After three weeks he quit going down there. Sascha made him. Her egoism again, her stirring will, her defiance, of as much of life as she needed to defy. When he was in Millbrook he wasn't with her. And she knew Leary a little from Harvard and detested him and wouldn't go there herself. She got afraid for Harry, not because she knew much about LSD—none of us did, except through him, and he was so understated about whatever he did that we never got that full reverent sense of its phantasmagoric properties that a few years later everyone in the world sported like this year's T-shirt—she just figured if Leary was promoting it, it had to be no good.

It was as easy for Harry to stop going to Millbrook as to start. He was probably the least addictive personality I'd ever known. His only addiction that I ever saw was for Sascha. So why do I mention any of this? To show my friend in one more vanguard, as if being first in so many things meant he must have been a born leader? Maybe, probably, in part. To show his adventuresomeness? Also that. I admired it, envied it, couldn't hope to match it. When I heard something new that Harry had done it was as if I could feel my bones and heart and knew they were not as strong as his. To paraphrase something I once heard a TV preacher say about Jews and money, he took more chances before the rest of us got out of bed in the morning than we did all day long.

On the other hand, Harry wasn't one of those guys, "You know me, I'll try anything once." He had a conservative bent, he ignored or kept away from stuff that was stupid, bad taste, or boring, and it's possible that innate upperclass sense of what passed and what didn't would one day save his electoral possibilities. You could never imagine Harry getting caught in a vice trap, or people thinking he was un-American for sampling a few pharmaceuticals. He would charm his way out of it, laugh his opponents into a corner. He could out-American mostly everybody, with his crewcut, his beachy twang, his dimpled chin and effortless affability. But he was counterphobic, if I understand that word correctly.

That's mainly, I think, what I'm trying to remember about him here. He was the biggest counterphobe I'd met. Since he couldn't bear to be beholden to it, fear became his ultimate guide, his ticket to freedom. When he felt it, he went in the direction that made it stronger, until whatever it was telling him he was afraid of was so close up, so overblown, it looked like a joke, like a big fish's mouth, yawning, white teeth filed, big fish's toothpaste smile, in a cartoon.

*Harry in the Political Union making a definitive statement in front of his father.*

The punchline first. Harry got up in front of about three hundred people after his father had delivered some starchy speech about our obligations to our neighbors in Latin America, and mooned the room.

But there was more to it than that. It was actually, from a debating point of view, a shot through the heart. In the Political Union they were often resolving some dubious proposition and arguing it in an arch and languid manner as they must have imagined was done by the debating societies of the only place Yale guys felt inferior to, Oxford. The night that Senator Nolan spoke he stayed on for the debate, which was something like, "Resolved, symbolic speech deserves free speech protection under the Constitution."

So what was a boy to do if he had the affirmative on that proposition, but get up there, yank at his belt, let his pants drop down, show his buns to all concerned, and get out of there without uttering a word?

If that wasn't symbolic speech, what was?

And if they laughed? Shouldn't laughter always be protected?

Case closed ipso facto Q.E.D. habeas corpus delecti.

There were those that night who swore that Harry had a bull-dog tatooed on his ass. But I'd seen Harry drop trou a score of times and never saw a bulldog, so if it was there it had to be a decal. George Shultz, on the other hand. Remember him? Secretary of State under Reagan. George Shultz went to Princeton and was said to have a tiger on his ass, and as far as I know he never even bothered to deny it.

Styles of the times. Teddy dropped trou once in a while, and so did Cord, and even I did a couple of times, mostly to show I knew how. But with Harry it was a kind of passion. It really was his free speech. Defiant, funny, friendly, gross. When he was asked about his son's performance in the debate, Senator Nolan said that it was succinct and persuasive. The judges had less of a sense of humor and disqualified him.

This was in the winter of our senior year. And did Senator Nolan have another conversation with his son that night or the next? In which the subject of his service came up? In which he was reminded what was necessary and what could be done and who could be called and that there were a lot of things you could do in the military, you could do intelligence, you could learn film, or read the news on the radio, or write propaganda leaflets. You could hook up with A.I.D. You could work on psy ops. You could win hearts and minds. You could get into the Air National Guard and keep the skies of Texas safe from the Vietcong air force. You could march around the 94th Street Armory on the weekend. You didn't have to get shot at.

Scenes I never saw. That require reconstruction, guesswork, sympathy.

Do I have such sympathy, or is it only a trickle, enough to identify and feel self-satisfied about, enough to serve my own purposes? It's why, of course, I admire Harry to this day. With him sympathy would be no question. It flowed out of him like a big river. In my mind, at least. The legendary, sort of, Harry Nolan.


\*


Harry as my friend, a primer, in images.

He was like Alexander and I was like his Aristotle. I tutored him here and there, I stayed up late with him, listening, reading his papers that had knit up his brow at three in the morning and making suggestions. It was amazing to me how much he trusted me, as if I really had some answers, and after awhile with him I always came away half-accepting that I had. On this purely intellectual playing field we believed in one another, like a prince-and-his-tutor tag team. I realized Harry had a strong mind, he was thinking all the time but he was quiet about it and not quite sure. And he was impatient with it. He liked to drive fast and his mind was like his car.

He was like America, and I was like a small convenient client state, maybe Israel. America loved me because I would do its bidding but also because I aspired to be like it, I really appreciated America, I saw its greatness, I was not one of those creepy little states that only wanted to take it to the cleaners. And America in turn protected me, lavished favors on me, spoke highly of me to the world.

He was godfather, I was consiglieri. He was chief, I was on the war council, patient, considered, cautious.

I was a mascot, of irregularity, proof of the ruling class's broad, generous reach. Mascots are often funny-looking, or anyway odd. Yale's bulldog. Tigers with funny smiles or birds with big feet and beaks.

I was the kid, still with a lot to learn.

I was Louie, a nickname, a baptized one.

The fact is it was only blind luck that I roomed with Harry at all. The rooms Harry, Cord, and Teddy were to live in sophomore year had a fire in them in August. Painters, cigarettes, turpentine. So they had no place to live and I had too big a place because my intended roommate decided he was lonesome for Texas and transferred to Rice. It was really the dean who put us together.

Although I suppose, after a little while, it was Harry, with his democratic impulse, who wanted me there. His democratic impulse: one part love, openness, optimism, his sense of justice; one part egoism, narcissism, ambition.

The sound of Harry as friend, "Hey Louie, come on, let's go," "Hey Louie, you asleep?" "Louie, you douche," "Louie, you fuck," "This is my friend, this is Louie." The world's tit-for-tat, like its laws of gravity, for a few moments suspended.

\*

Possible flaw (observed long ago) in the meritocratic theory:

That those who were raised up and given their big chance would have only their own interests at heart, that cleverness was no guarantee of character, that they'd give nothing back.

*

Harry as my friend, a primer, one more image:

He was the guy and I was the guy who had to be there so there'd be somebody someday to tell the guy's story.

# CHAPTER 9

It was the last night of the fair in Blue Hill. Cord wanted to show it to us because it was an old fair and the one where Wilbur the pig was headed in *Charlotte's Web* and it was a place for fried dough. There was something wrong with the Aston Martin. Harry said he thought it was the oil pump and he didn't want to run it till Monday, so we drove over there packed again into the F-85. It was about a half-hour drive.

The fair was a lake of colored lights in the country, sitting under the black shadow of the hill. It was stock car night and the race and rage of the cars filled the grandstand and the narrow lanes of food concessions and carny games with an incessant metallic groaning. The crowds flowed like fleshy lava through the lanes, people who worked all week or stayed home all week, people who'd been brought out for the first time in a month, people from "homes" and asylums, people from halfway houses, inland people, poor people, ordinary people, people fat on the fried dough of their whole lives, kids, babies, pregnant wives.

Teddy kept an eye out for free girls, but the pickings were slimmer than a starving Armenian, to quote one of the barkers who caught Teddy's roving glance. We got jostled by the crowd. We were a little crowd ourselves, meandering, leaning, getting lost from one another. There was a dithyrambic energy to the night. We ate ourselves silly when we were already stuffed, as though this was going to be the last pig-out of our lives. Fried dough, cotton candy, fries, onions, custard. We walked around with food in our hands like two-fisted gunmen. "No really, can ptomaine get you out of the army?" Teddy asked. "I mean, if it was a *really* serious case. Like if it lasted for three months or something." The evening turned cooler. Sascha wrapped herself in her sweatshirt and put her hands inside her sleeves. We lost about nineteen times trying to knock down three milk bottles and Sascha didn't want the prize anyway. What was she going to do with a plush zebra the size of a golden retriever?

Or for that matter a Baltimore Orioles hat, but she won that one on her own, at a pitching cage where you were supposed to guess the speed of your own throw. The rest of us were off by miles, always high. But Sascha guessed low. She threw an awkward slow girlish lob that barely got to the back of the net. Twenty-two miles an hour. On the button. She didn't giggle when she won. She didn't even smile. She had the brave, slightly perplexed, slightly embarrassed look of someone who'd just saved somebody's life. It was the only thing any of us won all night. The barker talked to her in the third person. What would the little lady like? He had a kind of bemused leer, and the sly, unshaven look of porn stars of a decade later. He asked all the rest of us weren't we ashamed, the little lady was the only one to win in an hour, who was going to step up and save the honor of the male race? Sascha had her choice of any hat on the top row, all the big league hats. She asked for the one that had the little bird on it, the oriole, with the orange wing.

She loved the color orange. An oriole's wing, a breadbox that was orange. In Cambridge she had an orange jeep. Anything else about her? While we're on the subject? Of her, her greatness, her winning ways, her lack of smiles. She always used too few words, and her voice was low and hard to hear sometimes. Her breasts were small. She wore mostly men's shirts. She knew things were easy for her and that she was patronized often, but she didn't blame people, she didn't think it was their fault that she was pretty and connected and rich. She believed that people exaggerated her gifts. She believed her real gift was something careful, patient and small, that few people ever saw. I could go on. I could get sidetracked. Her little brother who was thirteen. Maisie her sister. Her family were her best friends. At Harvard women crowded around her but she stayed aloof. And why did she love Harry? She told me once she didn't know why. I thought it was the first lie she'd ever told me, but maybe it wasn't.

His sweetness, maybe. His suitability. Mirror of her soul. A leonine sweetness, found at the heart of a roar, and not really a sweetness at all. A fearful symmetry.

Who the fuck knew. If you try harder do you think you'll discover it? Do you think trying harder is the key to the universe? You meliorist, you capitalist, you dull Johnny, is what being around Sascha made a boy think.

The fair with its country poor and cheap thrills had the odd effect of relaxing me, as if I were somehow closer to home, as if we were all proletarians now. I became aware of having been in a kind of slump with my friends, wary, unfunny, like a kid at a new school who doesn't know yet what to say, but away from the summer house, away from the rich people's weekend, the slump dissipated and I was for a little while wry and whimsical and quietly sarcastic, which was my version of funny. I could make a symphony of the word nice, a dozen tones, a dozen meanings, a dozen ways to raise an eyebrow, a thousand variations on a theme. The popcorn guy who picks his nose before filling Teddy's bag. Nice. The rubber worm that Cord won for only eleven dollars of SkeeBall. Nice. My own cotton candy mustache, that I didn't know I had until I saw it, as big and fat as a whore's mouth in a German expressionist's dream, in the fun-house mirror. Really nice. I never felt happier than when I could direct my friends' attention with some monosyllabic comment, and I played the comment and their laugh over and over again like a needle stuck in the turntable of my mind.

The rides flanked a wider, muddy promenade. A rickety ferris wheel, carny lights, thick electrical cords snaking the ground, things that went round and things that went up and down. Cord spotted three chone. "Chone" was a word that year. A hundred words for girl. The girls had round faces and cute hair and one of them wore a UMaine zipper jacket. They were going on the bumper cars, so that's where we went. Sascha found the naked chase amusing. Harry looked edgy, as though the presence of these girls might somehow slant the conversation in the direction of his talent for streetmeat. He said nothing to the girls. He paid extra attention to Sascha. Like Claude Rains in *Casablanca* he was shocked, shocked. By now Teddy had gotten their names. Maureen and Annie and Jackie. Catholic girls, French-Canadian, a couple of them anyway, with broad local accents that lacked *r*'s. I felt stupid chasing girls when Sascha was around. She would see what a revelation I was, me of the wise and judicious and sensitive demeanor with which I'd so often plied her. But she looked mostly wry. So this is what boys do.

It was a small rink for the bumper cars, the kind that could be packed and unpacked at every step on the carny tour, with faded hand-lettered one-way signs that everyone ignored. There were kids and dads on the ride, a couple of boyfriends and girl-friends, and an obese guy who let his hand dangle on the glassy metal floor as though this were very cool. And we slummers of the ruling class, and the girls. A simple seduction. You beat the shit out of the girl's car with yours as often as you could. Maybe the first seduction to be learned in country America, even the eight-year-old boys were bashing the cars of the eight-year-old girls. Sascha looked slightly surprised, as she had a tendency to look whenever she did something that ordinary people did, as if she didn't know quite how but was game to learn. I didn't see her smack into anybody hard. She was playing a polite game, and when the cars stopped she left.

The rest of us stayed on, even Bloch, though who was his chone?

The cars went around again, in a dance of sparks and ozone. It was becoming apparent that Jackie, the one in the zipper jacket, was mine. I bumped Jackie a couple of times to show my interest. It was a very small interest, and she may have seen it. One of the times around I could see Sascha across the prom-enade. I saw the back of the cap that she still wore and she seemed to walk slowly, beyond the crowd. There was a bench in the scruffy grass. I missed whatever happened next because I was going the wrong way but when I came back around she was sit-ting on the bench, her face mottled by the colors from a strand of high overhead lights. For a moment I only watched her. She got off the bench and sat in the scruffy grass. It seemed inexpli-cable, why she moved from the bench to the grass, and then she was lost to me again and when I came back around I could see she was pulling out grass and rubbing it on her face, as though to cool it, for the tactile sensation, or who knew why. What it reminded me of was a dog eating grass when it's sick. Yet so beautiful, she was so beautiful, sitting in the darkened patch alone.

Again I went around like a kid on a merry-go-round, Jackie bumped me lightly and snickered my way and I hated her for it.

Then I thought I saw Sascha crying. I could have been wrong. The colored lights made puddled reflections in her eyes. She didn't touch her eyes. She sat and rubbed the grass across her mouth. Harry saw it too. He got out of his car and slid across the slick floor, dodging and kicking at the other cars, the operator yelling curses at him.

All of this to me was like a movie with many frames missing. The next I saw he was sitting beside her in the grass. His legs were crossed. It looked like he was speaking, and then she lowered her head toward him. He took off her hat and held it in his hand. They sat there a long while without speaking, like figures in a sad billboard.

And then we were all leaving the fair. Teddy and Cord had made their case to Annie and Maureen. The girls wanted to go to a roadhouse, or anyway Annie and Maureen did, and they seemed to be in charge. Jackie was more the follower, the quiet one, content to do whatever, to be along. There was some talk of taking the rest of us back to Clements Cove and then meeting up with them. The talk about car arrangements soon got complicated, the way those conversations always seemed to.

But Sascha was revived by the idea of a roadhouse. She wanted to go. Mostly, I think, she wanted distraction, and watching Cord and Teddy work on "chone" must have seemed like a distraction.

And plain, quiet Jackie and I, were we an item too? It occurred to me maybe Sascha thought Jackie was the right sort of girl for me. Not as great a girl, perhaps, as I might have wanted but one who fit into the scheme of things, and as for my painful self-inflation well I'd just have to live with it.

We walked out of the fair and into the parking lot, which was in a muddy, tracked-up field. The girls gave us directions and waved us off. Their car was parked out on the road.

We continued walking toward the F-85. I was beside Sascha and for no seeming reason she took my hand. Her other hand was in Harry's. The three of us walked along. Her palm was dry and warm. For a moment I felt like we were in *Jules and Jim* but then I struggled with my sweet curdled silly and dishonest self, my self that placed myself in films. She liked me. They liked me. That was enough. God bless their union, or whatever pious people might say. Harry said, "I really want to get drunk tonight."

"I do too," Sascha said, and let my hand go.

# CHAPTER 10

Scenes that never were.

Turgid arguments over the correctness of the draft. Spirited arguments over the correctness of the draft. Hatching plans to go to Canada or underground or join some radical group.

Cooking up this thing that Al Gore had, where he was against the war but he was even more against having some poor kid from his draft board go in his place. A neat package, morality and viability retained in a deft stroke.

But Gore was later. Gore was in a tougher spot. Harry didn't really hate the war until he got to Ft. Ord.

And I'm unfair to Gore. I don't know the guy. I don't know if he cooked it up or not. I only know that Harry did not.

Another scene that never was. Harry telling me that he knew that I loved Sascha and that it was okay and that he was sorry, and gripping my shoulder shaking it slightly or the back of my neck in a way meant to help me move on. Because what else could he do but move me on?

Another: Harry telling Sascha about all the townies he had his way with. Yeah sure, he was just about to. But I almost did. During junior year, when they broke up for awhile. I thought he was being unfair to her and I thought she should know. Telling, ingratiating, angling. Maybe all of those, and maybe worse. But of course I didn't. They were back together again before I could, and anyway I never would have. Oedipal terror. Respect. Love.

No Judas here. No Judas on this boy's watch. If there was one thing out of a trillion I would steer my life to avoid, wouldn't it be that?

Iago Cassius Judas Shylock Caliban all that's turned out badly. I flirt, I fly from it. Envy and despair.

Though that was also the time I came closest to making a pass at her. We were at the train station. She was going back to Boston. We were up on the platform, on one of the cold benches, the white cyclopean eye of the train already distantly down the track. The politenesses of the well-brought-up. "Louie, thanks for taking me to the train." Nada, nada. "Thanks for everything, really. This was a mess, wasn't it, Louie?" "I guess it was." The train's eye had reached the start of the platform. We could hear its bell and its diesel rumbling. I looked its way, past her, and she did, and I grabbed the handle of her bag. She was wearing an old bomber jacket, some uncle's real one, and she turned back to look at me when I didn't expect her to at all. I looked at her as though to ask, why is this, why are you doing this, why are your star-blue eyes on mine when the train is coming down the track, and I cocked my head slightly, and my lips parted slightly, and I composed a friendly sympathetic noncommittal smile but I could have tried to kiss her then. The train bell clanged again, louder now, more insistent, like a dinner bell rung by a bored and angry cook, and she turned because it was time or maybe because she'd seen my funny look. The next day Harry was in his Aston Martin on his way to Boston.

More scenes that never were. Harry being a prophet, seeing two years ahead, the dirty colonial war like a knife to our hearts, like a mirror to our bowels, we who thought little before killing, we who built all these bombs and planes in clean factories, we with our cockeyed myopic ideas of the world, our Manichaean ideas, our blacks and our whites and our swaggering fat murderous ways. Harry being a prophet, seeing thirty years ahead, the Clinton years, America the placid, spreading her bounteous dominion, still ripping up a few markets, still decimating a few native peoples, but if you'd asked the people themselves, asked them in Hanoi, asked them in Pleiku or Ho Chi Minh City, they'd have told you about America the land of freedom and movie stars and their relatives in Orange County who were sad but sending money back, and then . . . and then . . . the planes flying into buildings and the guy with the broken grin who used to watch Harry batting handballs around leading America back to war. America in peace and war, but mostly war.

But Harry was no more a prophet than he was an historian. In his administration he would have planned to have both, a Secretary of Prophecy and a Secretary of History and they would have sat across from one another and glared at each other and canceled each other out, all but a tiny residue, which Harry would have lifted off the table with his fingers like grains of salt and licked and gained wisdom from. What an administration it would have been, like the best of the *Wizard of Oz* and Mr. Smith Does D.C. An administration with no chip on its shoulder.

Another scene that never was, this one arch and melodramatic as the players themselves were not. Sascha telling him not to go into politics because it was a dirty game and it would take him from her and they had each other and maybe that wasn't enough but if they lost that they'd have nothing at all. And Harry saying what would he do then, what else could he do, which she had no answer to so they'd make love instead.

And then she would dream of Harry as a sculptor or Harry as a college professor or Harry sailing around the world in an open boat and none of them made any sense except maybe the sailing around the world but he would do that after, after he was president or whatever he would be, his beard would be white and their kid would be grown.

Did Sascha secretly love power? I never knew. But if I'd had to guess, no. She dreamed of amelioration, by whatever means.

Another scene that never was. Harry blaming the war on Johnson. Everyone blamed the war on bumbling hayseed Johnson. Kennedy had gotten us in but Kennedy would have got us out. Johnson wasn't smooth enough or clever enough or enough at home in the world. He didn't know a fucking thing about communists except what he was told. Everyone said that or thought that about Johnson, everyone I knew anyway. But I never heard Harry say it.

Anticolonialism anti-imperialism third world developing world national liberation. Harry read about those things, but he didn't talk about them. He was still mulling. He hadn't decided.

Anything else, or do we quit while we're ahead?

Harry at *Dr. Strangelove* the first night it came to New Haven, in the Roger Sherman Theatre in the second row because the place was thronged, and we all laughed our asses off and did Peter Sellers all the way home. But Harry didn't laugh at all. The rest of us living under our comfortable if slightly scratchy nihilist blankets, with our thin pillows of irony to give us rest. But Harry didn't, couldn't, live that way.

A naif, then? A big strong know-nothing naif out of California, as naive and clean as fresh grass, who didn't want the whole human race to be annihilated and really thought, sometime, somehow, that he could, he would, do something about it? Another scene that never was, when he told me this, in grave sincerity, while we were walking home from the gym. He told me things in grave sincerity from time to time and sometimes when we were walking from the gym, but never that.

Then why mention it at all and where does all this come from? Maybe it's but an article of faith, maybe it's a convenient narrative trick. I'm not allowed to rely on dreams, am I? Yet I dream of Harry on Chapel Street, marching on a Sunday with a ragtag bunch of lefties with whom otherwise he had little in common, in favor of nuclear reductions or a nuclear freeze or nuclear nonproliferation or something, a placard in his hands, his voice raised, the local TV capturing it or not. A dream, not a memory.

Scenes that never were. Harry acting like something was a crisis, Harry in "crisis mode," if what is meant by that is acting like an asshole because something's gone wrong. Harry getting sentimental about anything at all. Harry without an edge. Harry looking awkward on his feet.

Harry loving anyone but Sascha. Harry doubting that he loved Sascha, or doubting that he had the ability to love, or that he knew what love was, or that love existed. He didn't take things like that apart. He was too simple for that. His heart wasn't broken.

Harry pissing on someone's grave. Though it's what we said we would do, in a drunken stupor in the Heidelberg bar. If one of us died, at the funeral the others would piss on his grave. A silly solemn college kid pledge, and it had to be at the funeral.

You couldn't just wait to do it at night, and best of all, the preferred option, was on the open grave, before the dirt was on, so you could really water it well. But none of us had died.

Harry in drag. He didn't do drag.

Harry stoned. There wasn't really any marijuana around yet. Not at Yale, not in the towers of the meritocracy.

Harry in despair. For what? Why?

*

Did I love her so much that in a secret part of my bones I wanted Harry to go to Vietnam and get killed so that I could have her for myself? No. No I did not.

Did I love her so little that in a secret part of my bones I wanted Harry to go to Vietnam and get killed so that I could have her for myself? No. No I did not.

Did I have a clue as to what love is? Probably not.

Did I or could I analyze it take it apart put all the parts on the table and name them and oil them and see how they fitted together and make a chart for future purposes? No.

Was I smart enough to realize that might not have been the way to go about it anyway? Maybe. I don't know. Probably not.

Did I have this oceanic, obsessive feeling? Yes.

Was tenderness a part of this feeling? Yes.

Was compassion a part of it? I can't say.

Were aggression, regression, a vast laying waste of the whole universe, violence, taking, theft, cruelty, cunning and stupidity combined, a part of it? Yes.

Was guilt a part of it? Yes.

Did I love her as an extension of my love for Harry? No. Possibly. I'm not sure.

Did I love her more than I loved Harry? I don't know.

Did I have fantasies that it was I who had introduced them to each other, that my love for her had preexisted Harry's, but I'd kept it quiet, waiting my chance? Yes. And in the meantime he jumped in with both feet the way he always did everything and she responded and it was all there, done, a fait accompli, and I was gracious because it was meant to be? Yes. But did I still remember, in my fantasy, how it might have been otherwise? Yes. Did I invoke justice in my fantasy? Yes, and when I did I hated it and chased it away. Being, even in fantasy, insufficiently fantastical, or insufficiently obscene, to think justice had a role.

There is no justice in love. Forget how bad the schools are, it's the one thing we're always taught young.

And yet, it was the most just thing in the world that Harry and Sascha were together. Anyone could see it. It was the first thing people felt. The second being some version of his destiny, unless they knew him before they knew Sascha in which case it would be the other way around. One-two, two-one, either way.

The kernel of truth in my fantasy: I saw Sascha sitting in Sterling Library, reading a book, while I was working there, before I knew anything about her and Harry. They'd just met, through a cousin of hers in Cambridge who'd known Harry at prep school. He'd talked about her, hey Louie I met someone, this could be the one, those things that are such clichés but nobody ever comes up with really a better way to say them, and he talked about her looking French or Italian, but I still didn't know what she looked like. Then there was this girl sitting in the library, at one of the long tables, with her knees up, with dark hair and eyes like blue coals and a pencil, left-handed, and a mouth that turned slightly down at the corners and something erotic in her lanky, athletic indifference. I looked at her. Probably I stared. A little later Harry came in and sat down beside her. This also felt like destiny.

And as well it gave my soul proof that I didn't love her just because she was rich or because of her family or because Harry loved her. I loved her, in a sense, before I knew a thing about her.

\*

One possible rebuttal to the supposed flaw in the meritocratic theory: even if the clever kids chosen for advancement were predominantly selfish, they would wind up helping others by helping themselves, exemplary players in the capitalist drama.

A second, more charitable, rebuttal to the supposed flaw in the meritocratic theory: clever kids weren't any more selfish than anyone else. If anything, they were more sensitive—and so more amenable to being inspired by the liberal canon, to the point where they could not only recognize superior character but have the imagination even to follow it, to put their cleverness into its service.

And anyway the meritocracy didn't want only the clever ones. It wanted the eagle scouts and the artists and the beautiful and anyone else who had *something* and maybe not the very rich per se but the buttressing, and very occasionally the grace, that all the money seemed to promise to buy.

\*

Class Poet Louie. Sascha called me that. And it was true, I was. A couple of poems, a prize. A giddy starlet's surprise, not entirely disingenuous. I felt I'd finally brought something home. A varsity letter, a merit badge. Something to put up on the scoreboard, Louie's contribution, March of senior year, at last. And would people see my talent now, the concealed burning of my heart? "Class Poet Louie." A joke in almost every way, because who gives a fuck who a "class poet" is, but on the flip side, Robert Penn Warren was the judge and Sascha seemed to think it was something. "Class Poet Louie." Her phrase, her greeting, the words champagne light and teasing on her softening lips. For a couple of weeks anyway. She wanted to know what my "class poem," to be delivered on "class day" in front of everybody, would be about. I never told her that, disguised in a hundred ways, it was of course about her.

# CHAPTER 11

We hit a few patches of fog but not many. The roadhouse was
back on Route 1, not a real log cabin but built to look like one,
with log siding and the logs overlapping in the joints like tightly
folded hands. A single streetlamp on a phone pole bathed the
trucks and beat-up sedans in the parking lot with a milky thin
light. The whole place hovered between the authentic and the
banal. A large Narragansett sign hung over the door like an asser-
tion of provincial propriety while the national beers, Schlitz and
Carlings, were consigned to twinkling in the narrow windows.
The bar itself was a sea of lumberjack shirts and flannel shirts
and T-shirts. As we walked in Cord made an anthropological ob-
servation about "Deer Isle smiles," where the locals' pants hung
so low you could see the crack of their ass, and a jukebox five
years behind the times played lyrics I'd rather have forgotten. It's
my party and I'll cry if I want to. The girl who sang that went to
Sarah Lawrence and people were always claiming to have fucked
her. Calumnies and lies. In my analysis of the universe the human

population would soon be down to zero, since all the people who said they were getting laid never actually were.

The girls had got there before us and had put two tables together in back. They ordered drinks with fruit juice in them and talked for ten minutes about their fake IDs. We were all twenty-one by then and around New Haven it seldom mattered anyway, a trip to the local package store was more a rite of passage into a universe of winks and nods than anything else, but Teddy paid a lot of earnest interest to Maureen's tale of having a friend who worked at the phone company where they had a Xerox machine and the tricks they were able to accomplish on her friend's breaks. She showed us her ID for the third time. A lot of talk about Xerox machines then, ending in Teddy bringing in his uncle who bought stock in the company when it was still something called Haloid and it went up six hundred times.

Thereby playing the inevitable but no less shameful for its inevitability money card that I was sure would come to a bad end somewhere, but the girls didn't seem to mind. If anything it spurred them on. Jackie replied that she had an uncle at Bangor Hydro and he bought shares in that and that went up too. Maybe not six hundred percent but it went up.

I thought of pointing out the difference between six hundred times and six hundred percent but I didn't want to sound like a pedant sweating the details.

Especially not on top of the preppie-pink shirt-J. Press–maybe-you-didn't-previously-notice-but-we're-so-far-above-you-we-could-spit-and-the-spit-would-evaporate-before-it-landed-on-your-heads dynamic that already seemed to be the alpha male weapon by default if not of choice around our two wobbly tables.

More than a little bit, I'm sure, when I start ladling out the irony, I'm reimagining these moments through Sascha's eyes. Even then I was pathetically sensitive to how she must have seen them. Did it make her more lonely? Did she even care? Sascha and Harry were hanging back like psychology majors doing the required field research for a course. And Adam Bloch was having a quiet night. He was acting as if he didn't want to make any more a fool of himself than he already had. Which wasn't so much, really, but he must have thought it was.

I was glad Sascha was drinking more, maybe she wouldn't notice as much. I drank a couple of gin-and-tonics quickly. Everyone else went through a couple as well, except for Bloch, who nursed a beer.

And as for the girls? Were backseat liaisons in the cards for us out-of-town princes that night?

The fact is, was, that preppies weren't really noted as cocksmen, to use a phrase that must have had more synonyms in Ivy vernacular than any other. It was true that preppies tended to get the cute preppie girls and made beautiful couples with them at Fence Club or in parking lot B on football weekends but by and large when it came to intersecting with the general female population in hopes of getting some, they were duds, a little on the slow side, encumbered by all the baggage of accents and manners and nonexperience, and overall a little English, if what you could mean by that was horny enough but shy. The rumor was that preppies grew up to be insurance executives and in a few instances homos and their cute preppie girlfriends grew up to be wives who shopped at Hammacher Schlemmer.

Harry on the other hand was a born cocksman. No eastern effete etiolation of the organ through guilt and too-careful breeding for him. And even I, despite all my desperate young Werther-ing in the direction of Sascha, had a certain potential in that area, in that I was shameless in the lies I could tell. Or at least I felt I could tell them. I hadn't often had the chance.

The problem, which I may have alluded to, was that Teddy and Cord, not to mention Harry, were by any culturally agreed-upon standard better looking than myself, and girls looked their way first. And they were rich and had other attributes. I am only expressing a wish, or a fantasy, which I held to dearly at age twenty-one, that if I didn't get Sascha, in the long run, as a kind of velvety consolation prize, I would get laid rather a lot.

And as for Teddy and Cord, they would or would not. Teddy could have turned out queer. Not a big chance, but some chance. We all vaguely sensed this, in the nervous unease he felt in his skin, as if he was always playing some game that he didn't entirely like. He turned certain situations caustic. Like he didn't have to mention the Haloid stock to Maureen. He was smart enough, he knew how obnoxious it would sound. But he was playing the game of being obnoxious, topping it all like an overrich dessert with cynical gloss. And Cord was too much a gentleman to be a cocksman. He was wonderful, he was charming, girls liked him and he liked them. But Cord was our Jimmy Carter who would tell them he had lust in his heart. He was, oddly, a kind of poet. If he'd had his chance at the Fireside Inn, he would probably have taken Annie out to the car and read her Marlowe, Christopher not Philip.

Also Cord was streaked with an indelible loyalty. To Harry, to Teddy, even to me. He would never steal a girl from any of us, or anybody else whose hand he'd ever shaken, and what kind of cocksman could you say that about?

But I love the concept. The three of us trying to get laid in our half-assed way, even on the weekend we were sending Harry away, even with Harry and Sascha sitting there.

But what else were we going to do? It was Saturday night and we were somewhere. Late adolescent boys fanning the flames of their last campfires.

Should we not have tried at all? Should we have been home with pipes and Monopoly games and earnest girlfriends we were trying to make a go with? I had my earnest love, sitting right across the table.

We got drunker and the girls wanted to know why we were here and Cord said it was because we were seeing Harry off into the service.

"Which service?" Maureen said.

"The Army," Harry said.

"My brother's in the Marines," she said. "Were you drafted?"

"Unh-uh. Enlisted."

"My brother was going to be drafted. So that's why he went in the Marines. Were you going to be drafted?" she asked.

"I don't know. Probably."

"My brother said at least if you enlist, you get your choice of some things."

"I guess that's so."

"But you have to be in three years instead of two."

"What's your brother doing?" Harry asked, and she told him about the Signal Corps and Camp Lejeune and how he might be home for Christmas, they were all hoping, and then Annie said her boyfriend was drafted in the Army, her old boyfriend from high school, and Harry asked her things about him too, where he was and what he was doing, and so the conversation became not about seduction, it lost its feints and jabs, it was about the things that were on their minds—in other words, it was seduction itself.

"So when you enlisted, what did you choose that you wanted to do?" Jackie asked.

"Nothing," Harry said.

Sascha sat there and didn't mind that he was the center of attention again.

His blue eyes hooded under his brow, his easy twang, his actual interest. He spoke so easily with them that the rest of us sitting there could almost imagine he was doing it to correct us, to show us how you talked to working-class girls or anybody else.

But he wasn't doing that. It was simpler than that.

"And where are you going?" Maureen asked Teddy.

"The Peace Corps."

"And you?"

"Business school," Cord said.

"And you?"

"I'm going to teach."

"And . . ."

"Grad school," said Adam Bloch.

It felt like the whole class telling about their summer vacation, but at the end of it the girls looked more troubled than enlightened. "I thought everybody had to go in the service," Maureen said, in a voice that hurt slightly.

"T. ey do," Cord said, "but not right away."

"And not if they get to be twenty-six," Teddy said.

But twenty-six seemed impossibly far away.

Annie changed the subject back to Harry. "So you didn't ask for, like *any*thing? I thought they gave you a questionnaire or something."

"I guess I like shooting people," Harry said.

"No. Really."

"I don't know."

"You'd be a good captain. You know, like an officer," Maureen said.

"No, you know what? You want to know really? This is all bullshit. I'm doing this for a really stupid reason."

It was then I realized he'd been drinking steadily, not a huge amount but not a little either. He'd told Sascha he wanted to get really drunk and he was anyway on his way. "If I told you I was going in the service because it was my duty, to serve the country, you'd say, good, right? But if I told you I was doing it so other people would see that I was doing my duty, so they wouldn't criticize me for not doing it, so they'd like me better, so they'd even vote for me if I was running for something—I mean, would *you* vote for me if that's what I was doing? I wouldn't. I wouldn't want a leader like that, a leader who thought that way. He wouldn't deserve it. He's the wrong guy."

The waitress delivered another round, the ritual that stops all barroom riffs cold, as money is fished for, who gets what is sorted out, bare fleshy arms stretch across tables and get in the way of faces. And then–

"But if you have to go anyway, what's the difference?" said Maureen, who was urgent, who really meant it, who was trying to save him now.

Harry's eyes sparked as he swung his head through the arc of light from the overhead. "Have to? Have to? Do these guys *have* to?"

Maureen was grazed. "So you don't feel any obligation at all to go in?"

"Yeah, no, I actually do. I do feel that. But that's only part. I don't want to get that part dirty."

"Everything's a little dirty," I said, thinking I was helping out.

"'The fuck asked you? Jesus Christ!" He glared at me as if he would murder me and the table quieted down. Harry pulled at his new gin and then he said in a low disgusted voice, "Fuck it. I'm not going."

Maureen was probably the only one at the table to take those words seriously. "You already enlisted. How can you get out of it?"

"His father's a senator," Teddy said.

"He is? Really?" Annie said.

"I'm more cynical than they are," Harry said. "They're at least doing something they believe in. I'm doing something so that people will think I'm doing something I believe in, so I can do something else."

"You like the idea of the Army," Cord said.

"Fuck it. Let Louie go in his place," Teddy said, and I wondered where that came from.

Harry sat back, closer to Sascha. His words left an echoey space that we didn't know how to fill. The girls shifted in their chairs and said a few words to one another in lowered tones. We knew we were losing them before they were lost, it was too uncomfortable for all of us now, and they took the last long sips of their drinks, fond and final, and got up to leave. They wanted to give us their phone number, they said. They wanted us to call them up. Teddy gallantly tried to explain how that could be difficult, since we didn't really live in Maine and wouldn't really be back, so maybe it would be better if they wanted to know us better to get to know us better that night.

But his heart wasn't in it. For a moment only Harry's was. Cord came back, Cord could call them, he said, and he was grinning then, and none of us knew why after what he'd said before.

The girls said their good-byes more to Harry than to the rest of us and then they were gone. He was still grinning as though to say what losers we were and how he could have shown us how to do this correctly with two hands tied behind his back and his cock in a brace but not, unfortunately, with his beloved bride sitting next to him.

For the moment his melancholy, his anger, his new resolve, were gone, a squall that came and went. When he was drunk, his moods were like rockets.

It was later still that the rest of us realized why we'd picked up the girls. It was to avoid, one, melancholy, two, sentimental recountings of past exploits, three, lies about the immediate future, and four, fear. All of them crept back at us as soon as we were drunk enough and alone.

Even I opened my mouth, with the longish story about the first time I saw any of these guys, when they busted through the firedoors of my freshman room chasing a rat with a pair of squash racquets, and what total preppie assholes my freshman roommates who were from the midwest and Texas and I thought they were and how we sent over a delegation demanding reparations on the firedoor, which the building inspector had blamed on us, and I expected they would have forgotten this, and they had. And later that year, when I was doing my bursary job in the library, how I'd helped Harry through Leibniz and Kant when I didn't know the first thing about either one of them except that they were the better sort of dead Germans. The best of all possible worlds, yeah right. The joke being on me, I supposed. Was that the point of it all? Or was the point that I could finally say to them I'd once hated them?

Harry had looked at me with murderous eyes and that was frightening but normal. But what Teddy said, I still wondered what that was about and maybe was trying to assuage it, to pass it off or pretend it hadn't been said.

Nostalgia night continued. Names of flamers, good guys, weenies, saints, tubesteaks, townies, thieves, bookies, hangers-on, various faculty and their notable perversions, were dredged up and polished like family silver recovered from a shipwreck. Only the last names, always the last names.

But things that had been funny were no longer quite as funny. We could feel this. We began to feel older. We began to feel as if we were living in the past, which was of course the whole point of it, to live in the past a little while longer, but it's one of those things you only become aware of the moment you've turned away, and when we turned, what did we see?

It got blurry. Whatever was out there was like the fog.

We laughed about standing on the bell.

I wished Bloch too would drink but he nursed his Schlitz.

I wished Harry would say anything at all, because he was quiet again and what if he still believed those things he'd proclaimed?

And then Sascha said, "I don't believe this is happening." She hadn't said anything at all until then.

Nobody, not even Harry, asked her what it was she didn't believe was happening. We sat there quietly as if a seer had spoken.

"We shouldn't have gotten married. Why did we? We shouldn't have. This is ridiculous. How could I have been this stupid? How could we have been this stupid?" She was speaking in a low voice with little inflection, in sentences so short it seemed like each one was separate, considered, a whole thought, a whole wound. "None of this is necessary. You don't have to go. I don't have to be here. None of us has to. Vietnam doesn't even exist. It's an

optical illusion. The army's an optical illusion. Why didn't we see it before? This is so stupid. We're so far behind. I stopped reading the papers. You know why? Because there was nothing about mirages in them. Why is that? It's so stupid. Really. Don't you agree?"

I don't know if Harry even cleared his throat, and then she said, still in a low voice with little inflection, "Of course you don't. You never agree with me. Nobody does anymore. I see all these mirages. But why? Why did we get married if it was an optical illusion? You think ... I don't know what ... but I'm going to study it in med school. It's in organic chemistry. Really it is. Organic mirages. They come and go in the morning."

I remember all these words she said. Well, maybe I've reconstructed a few.

It was all she said then. Really it was like the pythoness of Delphi or something. But she didn't get excited at all. She was speaking to Harry as if they were having a normal conversation, and I'm sure she was answering somehow what he said before, but the connection seemed clouded, obscure.

He didn't seem surprised.

Maybe it was because we'd all drunk so much. Four or five rounds except for Bloch with his Schlitz.

A little later we stumbled out of the bar. "I'm not going," Harry said again when we were outside. But there was neither affect to it nor context and no one asked him what he meant or where it was he wasn't going, so it just hung there and we didn't know. It was like a cold that had come back.

Bloch offered to drive because he was the only one sober. The night had gotten warmer instead of cooler and the parking lot smelled of marsh and diesel. It may have been two in the morning. The streetlamp over the parking lot was lost in blips of mist but the road was clear. Cord had the keys and was going to drive himself but Bloch asked again. It was like he'd saved himself, the sage, the designated driver, boring work but somebody had to do it, and why not he who'd humiliated himself playing touch football and wasn't even worthy of getting shot down by a bunch of townies from Bangor? A little act of redemption. Bloch had been saving himself for this, nursing his Schlitz, and anyway it made sense.

Cord gave him directions, which were to go a long distance down 15 past Blue Hill and when he got to a "T" take a right and wake Cord up.

We arranged ourselves back into the F-85, Cord and Teddy and I in back and Sascha between Bloch and Harry.

We went a little ways down Route 1 and then we turned onto the other road and we all fell asleep but Bloch. The road rollercoastered up and down the way it had the night before and it lulled me almost as if we were on a train. Sascha is a little crazy, is what I thought in a sort of dream, Sascha is a little mad or at least very much drunk and why not, I loved her for it, I loved her being a little teched, mad like Ophelia. In my dream I preferred it to very much drunk, more cosmic than very much drunk, more potent yet more fragile. Sascha with her restless hair and low, even voice, in the seat just in front of me, which when I thought it or dreamed it caused me to open my eyes, but I could no longer see her head because she'd put it in Harry's lap. I dozed again thinking of Harry and Leibniz and the best of all possible worlds, not that the world itself was that way, but the beauty of the words which for a moment made it almost so, and Harry looking at me with murderous eyes when I'd only tried to help. Everything's a little dirty. It's true, it's true, I pleaded in my dream. How inarguable is that, even Leibniz wouldn't argue with that, but Harry knew what he knew and he had a wish to be clean. Then I felt Cord who was next to me leaning forward and I heard him say in a gin-drenched but polite tone, "Don't put your brights on. It's better without the brights," and I felt uneasy and opened my eyes because I knew those words meant the fog was back.

Bloch had slowed down. He had both hands near the top of the wheel like they teach you in driving school, ten before two, ten after ten, and his shoulders looked rigid and I caught his hawk-like eyes in the rearview. The fog swept by us and for a little while it was gone and Bloch put his brights back on and the road opened up and then we went into it again. I was drunk but not so drunk as not to pay attention. It became like a contest between us and the fog to get us home, and I didn't trust Bloch though I saw he was doing his best.

We went past the fair that was dark now and the hill and Blue Hill village with its gas station and shuttered storefronts and church in the New England style like a ghost in the dark, and in none of those places was there any fog so I dozed off again.

I dreamed sweetly again, Harry had gone off to the war after all but now he was home and we were all singing with preposterous grand enthusiasm *The Battle Cry of Freedom* or at least the part when Johnny comes marching home again, hurrah, hurrah, a song he told me once he'd loved as a boy, and when I awoke it was because the car seemed to have shifted somehow. I heard Bloch say "deer," but I didn't see a deer, he yanked the wheel back too late from the other way that he'd already yanked it and we were off the road hitting a rock that blasted a tire and we flipped but didn't go over and then all I saw was the boulder ahead of us.

# CHAPTER 12

It was like a wonderment at first. So this is what something like this is, so this is what this is. A crash, this is a crash, we're already off the road. It was all going to happen too fast. There wasn't time to shout.

Teddy and Cord woke up soupy and dazed but trying to brace themselves and Teddy tried to curl himself and I felt myself between them and saw the tops of Bloch's fingers yanking the wheel one more time but either the car had left the ground or it was too close and it hit the boulder almost dead on.

In the backseat we were thrown forward against the front seats. We were debris, gravitation had no pull. I couldn't see Harry or Sascha. I don't remember any pain. The engine caught fire. I was conscious. Now I heard Harry shouting shit and Jesus and pushing against the door that wouldn't open. I still couldn't see Sascha but I heard him say her name. He was ramming the door with his shoulder and cradling her head with one hand but then it seemed that he let her go so that he could ram the door with all of his force.

Teddy managed to twist around and get one of the zippers to the rear window open and I twisted around and got the other, then we launched ourselves one at a time through the narrow passage as if we were triplets being born and slid down the trunk onto the ground. Cord's face was streaked with blood but I couldn't see from where. We went around the car. Teddy helped Bloch out the driver side while Cord and I pulled on the passenger door as Harry kicked it and shouldered it until finally it creaked open.

I saw Sascha then. One side of her face was bloody. She wasn't conscious. Harry got under her arms as if lifting a child and eased her from the car and I took her legs, which were warm and still and as normal as sleep, and we put her down on the ground. But the engine was still flaming, so we lifted her a second time to move her farther from the car. We all moved farther from the car.

All this time I felt nothing but the need to stay alive, like something that's always on but you never hear, an electric current or a rain when it's rained for days, pouring down now, the need for all of us to stay alive.

Harry knelt down over her, put his face close to hers and his hands on her cheeks and throat and breathed into her mouth or kissed her, I wasn't sure. I couldn't see her face. What had happened began to dawn on me but all of it had already dawned on him.

She must have still been sleeping and he was sleeping and maybe the bumps of going off the road had begun to awaken them but not enough. When we hit the great rock her head went into the dashboard, into the glove compartment or the vent knobs. Dashboards were metal then.

Teddy and I ran to the road. In back of us the flames from the car reached higher. In the fog they glowed, their light diffuse, like a fire inside a tent.

I thought to myself it will set the woods on fire but then I remembered it wasn't in a woods it was in a scrubby field with rocks and I asked myself if scrubby fields with rocks caught on fire and I didn't know the answer.

It was then I became so afraid for Sascha I had trouble getting a breath.

Teddy wavered like a pendulum and waited for a car.

I shouted that we should move Sascha still farther from the car. One of the few times I ever told Harry what to do. He lifted her up, alone this time, like a man with his bride in a movie when she is young and dying. He brought her toward the road and laid her down again. She was breathing, he said, and then he said it again.

He had blood on his arms and face. Cord ran up the road looking for a house and Teddy went the other direction. It was almost three o'clock, but I'm not sure I knew it or thought of it or of how slim were the chances of a car. None of us talked, except to shout at the world for help, and that we were here, and was there anyone around.

The gas tank went off with a rupturing thud and the car burned brighter and higher but the blueberry scrub didn't catch.

I began to feel a stinging on my face. I touched around and there was blood coming from my hairline.

Bloch was also around, in a daze, saying again that there had been a deer, he had seen a deer. I didn't say I hadn't seen it. I didn't say anything.

We could hear Teddy and Cord shouting, their voices like cotton in the fog, and then Cord seemed to shout louder so that he cut through the fog and maybe there was a second sound, of another voice or an engine's mutter, and I strained for the rhythm of a conversation, a back-and-forth of human voices or a car door cracking open. Now the fog in Cord's direction brightened like a thinning cloud with the sun behind it, swirled and confusing, and through it, as if our solar system had gained a second sun, came two beams of light. A pickup truck approached us.

There were a guy and his girl and the stuffed poodle they'd won at the fair in front and Cord jumped down from the truck bed. Teddy came running from the other way. I don't know if we'd all turned sober by then or were too drunk to know the difference. The guy and the girl looked like they'd been out screwing, there was grass in her hair and she looked swollen and his eyes were sweet and tired but he was a big guy and quick to help. He did some mechanics to get the passenger door to open and Harry laid Sascha on the seat and crouched down beside her in the space where you put your legs. The rest of us scrambled into the truck bed with the girl. The big guy climbed back behind the wheel, double-clutched in a show of ragged determination, made a U-turn in the fog, and we went off toward Blue Hill where they had the hospital. The car was still burning in the field.

He drove fast. We sat with our backs against the side of the truck bed and the fog flew past us like dreams. The girl sat in a corner, holding her prize from the fair between her legs as if she was afraid it would blow away. Bloch was across from us, so sober and unblinking he might have been in shock.

Though it was one of the things about Bloch, that he seldom blinked. He could out-stare anybody.

I prayed every second that Sascha was still alive. Every second, that is, that I wasn't cursing my inability to pray, the words seeming false and belated in my life, like who would believe me now.

In Blue Hill the fog was gone. The hospital seemed nearly shut. A pair of hundred watt bulbs were on where the sign said Emergency. The big guy honked mercilessly and Teddy ran inside bringing back two big-hipped nurses with a gurney. Everything seemed slow motion but I don't suppose it was.

The rest of us got out of the truck bed. I heard Harry say, to one of the nurses, that she was alive, that she'd hit her head.

I saw her then, as the nurses and a male attendant who also came out moved her onto the tray. Harry had put a towel from the car to the left side of her face, but around the towel her face looked dark, looked black-and-blue perhaps. She was as still as sleep, her eyes were shut. The male attendant laid a blanket over her.

I thought, as they wheeled her in, that she could have been going to have a baby.

But why did I think that? Harry's baby? Harry who was beside her, who followed the gurney as though he were a boy racing to keep up with a lover's departing train.

It was a country hospital and it was late at night and calls had to be made. We were the only emergency patients. There were cots and the nurses had been dozing on them. It was almost like a motel where you arrive late and wake up the attendant to ask for a room. They wheeled Sascha through white doors and down a corridor. Harry remained by her side. I heard one of the nurses phone the surgeon. Her accent was flat and heavy. A car crash and a girl with a head injury and how long and the phrase "fifteen minutes." The surgeon would have to drive over. More time,

more waiting, the loss of all context. I couldn't tell how long fifteen minutes was. It could have been all the time there ever was.
The nurse called the sheriff and the fire department. She cupped
the phone and asked Cord where the car was but he wasn't sure.
I went out and got the guy from the pickup truck and he told her,
such-and-such miles, so-and-so's farm. The room we were in was
a boxy, fluorescent-bathed space with plastic chairs in addition
to the cots. Not much medical equipment around; posters on the
wall concerning poison ivy and measles. All of us kept looking
through the small windows of the white swinging doors but there
was nothing down there but corridor. The other of the two husky
nurses began to examine us by turns, asking us to lie on one of
the cots while she probed with a portable light and cotton swabs.
We were told there was a doctor in attendance but he was with
Sascha. I kept looking at the clock until fifteen minutes were
gone. There was nothing wrong with any of us but bruises and
cuts, and Bloch had the least of all. It was kind of a miracle, the
nurse said. Bloch said that he'd been wearing a seat belt. We
looked at him strangely. "Were *you?*" he asked lamely, of Teddy,
of Cord, of any of us. "No," Cord said, and Bloch didn't know
what more to say, he nodded and put his hands in his pockets.

The surgeon arrived. By now I knew the time too well: twenty-
two minutes had passed. The surgeon drove an MG which he
parked in front. He was a horn-rimmed kind of guy who must
have moved here from somewhere, thinning hair, small nose. He
went past us in our piteous irrelevance and took both the nurses
with him, through the doors, down the corridor, off to the left
somewhere where Sascha was. All of this, at last, in a hurry.

We waited. Harry didn't come out. The sheriff's deputy
arrived, a guy in his twenties, brown uniform, sunken cheeks,
watery eyes, poor complexion. It was both relief and an irritation

to have him there, in that we hated to look down the corridor nor could we bear not to for more than a few seconds.

The deputy had his pad out and asked each of us some questions but he didn't take us one by one. We all stood around him like a basketball team with its coach. He wanted to know where we were going and how fast and where we'd been, our whole night, and was there liquor in the car and who was driving. Bloch said he was driving. The sheriff looked at his license and asked him if he'd had any alcoholic beverage to drink. Bloch said about three-quarters of one beer, and then—too much? was it always too much with Bloch?—that he was driving because he was the sober one. The deputy asked him how the accident happened. Bloch said, "I don't know. We were in fog and I saw a deer, so I swerved, I don't know. I swerved too far so I swerved back."

"Did you hit the deer?"

"No. I missed the deer."

"Did you know," the deputy said, "maybe not where you come from, but up here, when somebody has a crash and they say they swerved to miss a deer, it's usually believed that's a story to cover they were intoxicated."

"But I wasn't," Bloch said. "I only had three-quarters of a beer," and Teddy chipped in that that was so, and I did also, and Cord said he gave Bloch the keys because he knew he'd had less than one beer total.

Bloch offered to take a test. But he was acting sober and the deputy asked him to exhale and he smelled Bloch's breath and that was the end of that part of it.

Meanwhile Harry had not come out, nor either of the nurses.

The deputy wanted the owner of the vehicle to accompany him to the scene of the wreck, so Cord went with him. The wait became so unbearable it took on personality, like being strangled by someone you know.

And as I waited I began to thaw, began to have feeling again, and it dawned on my slow mind what "traumatized" meant. I, I was traumatized, self-anesthetized, and the anesthesia was wearing off. Sascha. Her name sibilant and soft, like furnishings in old homes. What was Sascha feeling? Her mind. Did Sascha's mind still exist? I felt the possibility like a flicker, then like a flash. Her injury. Was she in pain? Could Sascha live with pain?

In a weird jujitsu of feeling I could more easily imagine Sascha dead than in pain, because if she were dead, death not being real to me, it seemed a short jump back to life, but pain was just what it was.

I knew what pain was. Sascha in pain, Sascha in life, Sascha down the hall out of sight with strange men and women working over her and Harry for once in the span of my knowing him as helpless as a child.

Bloch sat in one of the plastic chairs with his hands folded, leaning forward, little Band-Aids on his hands, one ear, his chin.

Teddy and I stood around. I had a bandage on my forehead and he had something on his arm.

Life reduced to dazed, stripped moments, all that had gone before erased, history restarted on a bleak and ugly page.

We stayed quiet, even Teddy, who always had something to say. Were we strangers, after all?

In the silence I rehearsed words to say to Bloch, rehearsed them until they were sanded clean of my feelings, until what was left was something smooth and fraught, like a careful piece of work. I'm not sure I meant to say any of them, but then the waiting got too long. "You know, Adam, I kind of had my eyes open. I didn't see it."

He looked at me oddly, as though that was the oddest thing to say.

"The deer. I didn't see it," I repeated.

"Were you awake?"

"At the end. When you were losing control I was."

"It was there," he said.

"I didn't say it wasn't. I just . . ."

"It's why I swerved."

I could tell nothing about what Bloch was feeling then. He was like something that had petrified.

"So you were wearing a seat belt," I said finally.

"Yes."

"It's a good thing," I said. "Lucky thing."

"Was it?" he said.

Then we were quiet and I looked again through the swinging doors. Nothing more was down there than had been there before.

Teddy was looking at the pictures of poison ivy and poison oak and poison sumac on the wall. He was avoiding Bloch's glance, which I could see and it was pleading. And he was also, I thought, avoiding mine.

Bloch shuddered like a machine coming apart. Then he said to Teddy, or to both of us but he was looking Teddy's way, or maybe mostly to himself, "I was going to tell them they could put their seat belts on, too. I was trying to think of a funny way to say it. The captain has turned on the Fasten Seat Belt sign. Or offhand, like seat belts are in there somewhere if you want them, there's a little fog. You know. So they wouldn't think I was a flamer. So they wouldn't think I didn't know how to drive. Or I was bossing them around about something really stupid."

"You're a considerate fuck, aren't you," Teddy said.

# CHAPTER 13

My guilty secret about Bloch: I believed he was me. In some part of me each thing I ever saw Bloch do, each way he looked, what he said or failed to say, his crooked humor, his striving, his wish for validation, all me. I could see me taking the keys from Cord. I could see my humiliation at the goal line. I could imagine saying too many things and not knowing when to stop. I could imagine my hands on the wheel. I could imagine nursing a single beer. I could imagine the fog and not saying I didn't know how to drive in fog and putting on my seat belt and thinking that others should but not telling them so they wouldn't think I was an asshole. I could imagine myself frozen in fear. I could imagine my shoulders hunched. I could imagine all of these things more easily than I could imagine being anything like Harry. I could imagine my entire self as dull clay, yet a tremendous dream to be a hero. Grandiose fantasies of me, and a dull unblinking look, as though to ask how did I get here.

Scenes that never were. Bloch telling a joke. Bloch moving in a way that was graceful or natural. Bloch losing his temper or saying an unkind word or doing anything uncontrolled.

Are my characters getting away from me? Are they running into the ground?

Scenes that never were. Bloch giving up on himself. Bloch letting go.

Not this and not that. The sculptor chips away.

I could imagine seeing the deer. I could imagine the dark unfamiliar road, and my hands tightening. I could imagine the futility of my headlights, lighting up the clouds. I could imagine the deer, tremendous, bright, and leaping in front of me. I could imagine turning the wheel as if I were in snow in Rochester in January and I was sixteen years old and had been told if you skid to turn the wheel in the direction of the skid but it was so hard to believe, so counterintuitive, so full of a dangerous dare. I could imagine the deer dissolving in the fog but too late because I had turned too far. I could imagine still believing in the deer, still clinging to the deer.

But the deer was the light and the fog and I could imagine knowing this, somewhere in my dense soul.

I could imagine swearing never to admit it or think it for a very long while.

I could imagine turning the wheel back and bumping off the road and having no control at all.

I could imagine myself in my incompetence and helplessness and rage hurting her, hurting all of us, being the one, wrecking Cord's car, wrecking it all. I could imagine fucking up, and thinking of it that way, Bloch, you've fucked up now, Louie, you've fucked up now.

I could imagine my light-headedness. I could imagine wandering around and not knowing what came next in the world.

I could imagine being still behind the wheel and seeing Sascha's crushed face, what I had done, what the car had done, what the deer had done.

I could imagine wanting to cry, but not crying. Stiff upper lip, Adam. Stiff upper lip, Lou.

Isn't that how it's said in wartime films? Isn't that how men behave?

Years later I would feel the same about Nixon. When they were kicking Nixon around I would say to myself there's a lot of Nixon in me. I said that to Cord once, I thought it would astonish him. He said to me, "There's a little of Nixon in all of us. It's how he got elected." And he said: "But Nixon is all Nixon all the time, and you're not."

Proof that friends have wisdom, that you learn things from friends. Which as it happens is what I believed with my whole heart in the summer of 1966. I think we all did, as if in a Mafia movie where the first act they're all friends, and the first act never ends.

Third acts were only an hypothesis, distant and bloodless, like rumors of war.

No, I wasn't Bloch. But I felt as bad and as guilty as Bloch. Or maybe I didn't. Maybe I couldn't. Tend your own garden, Louie. Don't go looking for others' troubles. Harry might have said that, if the mood had hit him that way. The exact advice he would never have taken from anybody. He who was headed in the opposite direction from me, from Bloch. But we were together in the car that night. No, I wasn't Bloch. What he felt, the depths of what he felt, would be, on calm and measured authorial reassessment, obscene for me to assert, claim, announce, colonize, presume or for that matter a dozen other verbs. It is what it was. Imagination.

Scenes that never were. Bloch in the emergency room while we waited, coming up to Teddy or me with a broken heart. Bloch shouting or screaming. Bloch looking through those narrow windows, down into the empty corridor.

And another: any of us, myself, or Cord, or Teddy, saying to Harry, ever: you shouldn't have invited Bloch. You shouldn't have incorporated him, made him your friend, gone that mile too far. A tragic mistake, we never said. An overreaching, we never said. And if you hadn't . . .

\*

Meritocracy vs. democracy.

At the heart of democracy is equality for all, but in its operation is equal opportunity for all.

At the heart of meritocracy is equal opportunity for all, but in its operation is a picking and choosing, of those most worthy to advance.

Meritocracy is proud of its efficiency, its shrewd use of resources, its modernity, its fairness, its wisdom.

But democracy scorns such "advancement." What good is it? A man who is clever may become rich and enrich the nation, but he has no better chance of solving the existential riddle than a slow, plodding man. No better chance of behaving well in a car crash. No better chance of behaving well when pain and horror are let loose, when charity might be found or lost.

Meritocracy knows it has an answer to this, but it cannot think of it, or is afraid to say.

# CHAPTER 14

The three of us and Bloch. Or a stranger, a visitor, I suppose would have said the four of us, as a Venutian on late night TV would say earthlings, not Americans, Russians, Mexicans. No more words. The only time any of us said anything was when the terror of the silence got so big it filled every crack in the room, and we spoke to get a little space back to breathe. "The fuck they doing?" "The guy's good. He's from Mass. General." "There's some coffee."

More than an hour went by. Cord returned with the deputy, who seemed to have become his pal, or his worried guardian. "Anything?" Curt looks. "Harry's still in there." The deputy got Cord a cup of water from the cooler. Then he stood around with the rest of us like we were still his old team, until a call came in and he left.

At the end of the corridor we could see there was a second corridor to the left. It led to the operating room, but also offices and lockers. Harry was there, in one of the offices, out of sight.

Everything I can say about him now was from what he told us later. He had phoned New York and Sascha's father had in turn awakened her uncle, the one who was the heart surgeon at Columbia, and the uncle had spoken with the surgeon in Blue Hill and from all that was said Harry knew that the situation was grave, there was no question of moving her further, to Bangor or Boston, not for now anyway, there wasn't the time, there was no stability, the surgeon would have to go in now. These were things the surgeon had also told Harry directly, but when he heard them repeated on the phone between doctors he knew they were true, or anyway as true as the surgeon could represent them. The surgeon turned from peremptory and self-important to attentive and comradely after he learned who Sascha was and who they all were. Impressed by the Maclaren name, knew somebody who was somebody who knew somebody, and so it went even in the corridors of life and death. Harry disliked the man but Sascha's uncle said he seemed okay and his credentials were first-rate, better than you could have hoped for. Harry remained on the phone a little while, after the surgeon went in to do his work, and the uncle kept talking, about this and that, protocols and indications, which was a good thing, Harry thought, although he had trouble taking in the words. A good thing because Harry and Sascha's father were two men separated by a wire, Harry could imagine the plunge of the Maclarens' happiness and hopes more easily than he could imagine his own but he could say nothing about it that didn't sound ridiculous, nor could Sascha's father.

Harry, alone now, tried to will the phrase "head injury" into a shape he could understand, that images, thoughts, and hopes could adhere to like messages on a kiosk. If the doctor had meant something more serious would he not have used a more complicated phrase, but "head injury" was what he used. Even with

Sascha's uncle he said "head injury," though he used other words as well.

Harry didn't believe what he was thinking any more than he believed in spring training dreams. But he did, for a few moments, believe in his own dumb will. It was what other people always saw in him and he had never had much time for it himself, but it was all he had now. He could will "head injury" to be less than what it was. He could will "head injury" to be as benign as it sounded. Stitching, patches, scars, a little cosmetic surgery, unhappiness but life. You can't take someone like Sascha away. It's preposterous, it's unprepared for, there must be an appeal from this somewhere. A mistake has been made, like an error in celestial addition. But if we shut our eyes really really really hard . . .

Is this Harry, so desperate, so forlorn? Twenty-two years old.

Sascha, also, twenty-two years old.

Is it old or young?

Depends, I guess.

He willed the surgeon's hands and her protoplasm and her skin, healing up like a film running backward.

He willed her to pull through and to be fed an incredible amount of drugs so that her pain would be less but at last she would open her eyes and she'd be weak and her skin sallow and she'd hate food for awhile because of the drugs but others would come, her family, everyone would wait outside or come in for a few minutes at most on account of her weakness, but or until eventually when she would sip something, her lips would be moist and the IV would become obsolete and she'd watch a few minutes of TV before drifting off. That would be great, that would be everything he could wish for.

But no one came out.

He thought about Sascha's sister, Maisie, coming to visit, and her beautiful little brother.

And then what seemed a long time, as long as to cross a desert, all he could think about was the time he'd stood her up. They'd just met, this was in Cambridge, a complicated story with exculpatory factors but what it came down to when you rubbed away all the sly and pliant arguments for the defense was that Teddy had tickets to a Red Sox game. Yes, their plans (Harry and Sascha's) had been tentative, yes, he left a message. But her bristling rage. That's what he remembered. Her rage with the word *bristling* attached to it, compounded of her heart's opening to him and her hurt and her absolute conviction that once things are so far wrong they can never be made right, an omen, conclusive evidence, and her need to blame someone more than herself because she already blamed herself too much, for being in this fix, for liking the jocky bastard with his no-good western ways, for falling in love in a way no better than any other cliché. He showed up at six o'clock at her dorm, after the Red Sox had lost to the Yankees, and she was throwing stuff at him, phone books, she threw a phone book. That's what he kept remembering, not how they'd make love later in the bushes of the observatory.

Sascha wronged. What a concept. He almost laughed.

And then, as if on account of it, he had to believe in immortality. Not out of weakness, it seemed, but obviousness, a sort of force majeure, in which sometimes you give up and go with it like you're still on LSD, all manner of shit flying around including the truth if you can only find it.

Latch onto Sascha. If anybody can't die, she can't. Not with a bristling rage like that. Goddess Parvati dark-haired girl.

In her blood, in her corpuscles, this is where the battle is fought, house-to-house, hand-to-hand. Here Sascha wins. The territory of Sascha is inviolable. The territory of Sascha is immortal. There's a flag, there's *élan vital*, there's a song. They give up territory but they win it back. Valiant soldiers who sing her song and he, Harry, is one of them. He would die for her, for any and every inch of her.

Though later, when he told me these things, Harry also said that metaphors of war are horseshit. He wrote this to me from Ft. Ord. I thought it was so brilliant and I wondered if he'd heard it or read it. Metaphors of war are wrong for everything but war, he wrote. Everything else they mess up, they turn complication into this-or-that, one thing or the other, enemies.

Sascha was not an enemy of death. She would win finally in transcendence. There would be realms where he would find her, big realms, not little dinky ones like this room with a desk and a phone and a chart of what makes a person obese according to the Department of Agriculture. Harry went, while he waited for Sascha, from a psychologist's point of view, insane.

Realms of being that he'd only read about, he believed in. And then he came back, like a tumble at the end of a trip, with a headache and the headache's name was Adam Bloch.

He felt he shouldn't hate Bloch, for eminently practical reasons, because if he hated Bloch and it was not just, God might take it out on Sascha. He wanted to do nothing to alienate God. He wanted to be the best little boy he could be. Instead he blamed himself, for getting drunk, for letting her get drunk, for falling asleep, for not waking up. Where had his hand been? His hand could have saved her this. Why did he not always sleep with his hand on her face? Where had he been in his dreams to neglect it? An argument, a pledge, against dreams, ever, they're too dangerous to life. How could he have left her so, it was worse than going to that Red Sox-Yankees game.

But he knew Bloch had caused the crash. Lame evil weenie flamer who stares at you and doesn't even blink. Who couldn't save somebody's life, who couldn't even bring people home safe, who didn't even drink.

He tried so hard not to blame Bloch, for Sascha, for superstition or faith.

When the surgeon came out it was possible to know from his expression what had happened. Harry saw it but refused to accept it, because what if the surgeon was a man of head-fakes and feints and drama, or what would it mean if Harry plain guessed wrong, if he guessed his bride had died and she had not? He felt, somehow, that would be a crime. The surgeon's eyes making a point of not looking away. Pulling his cap off, rubbing his nose with his sleeve. "It was a serious head injury. We were unable to revive her, or help her." Harry heard the downward flow of the words.

He had never imagined that this small office with its metal desk and obesity chart would take on dimensions so definite in his life. The fluorescent light felt like the light of the whole world, thin and with a hum.

The surgeon's name was Cairns. He introduced himself, which he had done once before but it seemed forgotten. He said how sorry he was. Harry heard something kindly in his voice.

He went in to see her. His life was changed now. He knew this. Nothing else but this could have changed it. He kissed her face many times and held his cheek next to her cheek and imagined that she was smiling at him in a way that was sweet and overwhelming.

He lingered in the sweetness. The son they would not have. And her thoughts, what happened to them now, where did they go?

Lingering awhile. Let them say something, the hospital people, if he wasn't supposed to stay. Let them bring words in here, where they didn't belong.

Extinction. What sort of word is that?

Her cheek was cool.

Harry made a mental note to ask the doctor about her pain, what sort of pain she had had, and for a moment making such a mental note gave him strength, like an early sign that life would go on. But he soon forgot the mental note.

He didn't want life to go on.

It seemed like no one would come in to disturb him. He touched her legs, her feet, he pushed back her matted hair. He kissed her wound, where the surgeon had worked and left it dark and like a small worksite, a place of excavation.

Then one of the nurses came in, her white uniform like a badge of the world as it is, ongoing, time-deceived, and he went out to call New York and tell them.

It was the other nurse who informed the three of us. Teddy yelled "Shit!" and spun around. Cord hung his head, said a half-way audible prayer, his lips moving, his eyes squinted close to shut.

I don't know that I said anything at all. Nothing you could mark down, say was behavior. I felt inadequate to life. Both my parents were alive. I didn't know the laws of grief. What it would be, whatever it would be. The only thing I could compare it to was so stupid, but when I heard that Kennedy had died. Not when he was shot, but that little while afterward, when everybody was still hoping and then we heard.

I suppose I kept my counsel. I was afraid to speak, knew it would just be show. I waited for the next thing to happen.

Bloch started to walk away. I hadn't looked at him until then. He had a stumped, bewildered expression, someone who had caught the wrong train or a scientist with an experiment gone awry. I saw him blink. Now there was something. It was a slow blink, almost controlled, and he tried to look at all three of us, in succession, almost the way they must teach you in salesman school, get everybody in the room. But he was trying harder than that. He was trying hard to be real now. What could he say? He'd ruined his life. He'd crossed one of the only lines. "Tell Harry I'm sorry, okay?"

We could have said something. Any one of us could have but we didn't. We were pretending it was too hard, as if no words could suffice for the vast disappointment we felt. We glared, or looked away. What self-righteous bitches we were, but it was also true, in part, that we couldn't help ourselves. We had to do something. We could have hit him, but we didn't do that. A whiff of violence floated in the antiseptic air.

Bloch saw our contempt for what it was or pretended to be and said, "You want me to go kill myself. You want me to go jump in the river."

"There's no river out there," Cord said. "It's a bay."

"I get the idea. You don't have to be sarcastic." It was the only time I'd ever seen Bloch's eyes bright. Incandescent with crazy guy fearlessness. "I get the idea," he said again. "How about electricity? Would that be better? Electrocute myself? Slit my wrists? Get myself run over?"

"Adam, come on," I said. Then I said, "Nobody wants you to kill yourself, Adam," but what I really meant was that no one wanted the problems of it. About the rest I wasn't sure, I couldn't think.

"Thanks," Bloch said. "Thank you very much."

Were we utterly powerless in the face of Sascha's death? I think Bloch knew we were, but felt more powerless still. What destiny could he take charge of now? What transformation of self effect? The logic, the harsh, stilted rhetoric, of death.

"Where are you going, Adam?" Teddy said.

He was walking out of the hospital.

We looked at each other when he was gone, fleeting glances, but they showed no guilt.

A little later Harry came in through the white doors. His face was still not bandaged or washed. Marked with his blood or hers. We crowded around him and embraced him. He seemed then like a man who'd been pointing, looking, guarding, all his life in the wrong direction, and now he'd been called from another. Like a gun emplacement facing the sea, and then the enemy attacks by land. I felt an odd, light sensation, as if a wind was lifting me up.

"Where's Bloch?" he said.

"Out," I said. "He's in pretty bad shape. He's a little crazy."

"He said he was sorry," Teddy said.

# CHAPTER 15

Sascha. Outline of her, a little later in life. A doctor. In the field. In Lebanon or the hinterlands of New Mexico. Somebody Oriana Fallaci might have written about. Compassion and a certain hardiness, even resiliency, as if she'd grown up to be, surprise surprise, some species of beautiful weed, surviving drought and fire, indestructible. One who never watched TV.

Would their marriage have survived? All the marriages from that time, all the ones I ever heard of anyway, seem not to have. The wear-and-tear, the rough roads of all those years. Yet I can see them breaking up and getting together again. Getting married not two times but three. Something crazy, slightly mythic. Something that wouldn't keep him from getting elected because people would see what a miracle it was. Her work would keep her apart but bring glory and a touch of morality to them both. Someone taking on the heart of the world.

Sascha. Outline of her in middle age, in late middle age, as the third millennium of the Christian era begins. Her hair mostly white but still flying, and her eyebrows dark in dramatic contrast. Still in the field, here or there. Doctors Without Borders, maybe. A couple of kids, the girl at Harvard the boy off in South America somewhere. A couple weeks of Maine in the summer, where she's begun to sculpt. A more cheerful sort than she was; gives a lot of money away.

And if the White House thing really happened?

It feels a little kitschy but I'll get there. Not Jackie Eleanor Laura Ladybird Hillary, surely not Pat nor the others. Wretched job, best to ignore it but you can't. Embrace the capacity to do good, do what you can anyway. Forget the cheerleading, just the example. A little clinic somewhere in D.C. Every day to the office. Poor kids, kids with AIDS, bloated mothers, gunshot wounds. The run of the mill. And a TV show? "E.R." meets the White House?

Thirty-five years have passed and I remember her preciousness, her promise, her quiet, and yet the great galloping stride of her life.

The thought of her babies. Fat and ugly, born with a crewcut. How beautiful they would have been.

*

Am I exploiting my friends, dragging the gold out of their teeth?

Pitiless world, this meritocracy. More like a stampede, souls climbing over one another to be the first to die, capitalism's neatest, most efficient trick yet.

My friends were beautiful and I was sly, for it's I who write all this down.

Although how sly will I seem if my book sits in the second drawer from the bottom, where like a half-built bridge it currently resides, until I die and the desk is sold in the garage sale whereupon a lot of papers will have to go. Or do I presume to say . . . *estate* sale?

Then would I be a martyr, as much as they? They would still be beautiful. They would still give hope. But I would have failed them and failed myself and in the name of what?

I could have had a job all this time I've spent in my room. I could have been making good money. Lawyer, producer, scriptwriter, guy on the phone. I've done that stuff, I know how it goes. I could have been in the world, hurly-burly, getting laid.

Setting aside my friends for the moment, I seem to wish to be the poet of something that may not deserve it. Meritocracy. Hardly a poetic word. Neologisms seldom are.

Or, in a more considered view: the lives of those who deserved it all and didn't get it.

And the shouting of the Robespierres, why the fuck did they deserve it all in the first place, what romantic hooey is that, rose-tinted and touched with consumption, they *had* it all and *earned* nothing.

From the bitter ashes comes something glorious, and it's not wrapped in a flag.

Sascha. Outlines. The origins of my love for, or if you will, obsession with, her. A steady mind. A sturdy but turbulent heart.

The best are bright but not the brightest. The brightest are like those halogen headlights in cars, so bright with their silver-white light they make it harder for anyone else to see.

Big two-hearted rivers are what we need, the pledge of the words if not the story.

Sascha. Outlines of grief. I grieve, you grieve, we all fall down.

\*

A plot alternative, a plot possibility.

On account of Sascha's death, a brilliant career is derailed, Harry grows into the ways of the times, marches, black churches, a place in Vermont, he drops acid one hundred and seventy-eight days in a row but it does him little harm and a few years later he founds an ice cream factory or a fish farm and just when you think his political days are behind him, twenty years late, out of the ashes comes a candidacy, backed by all that ice cream money, which is fifty times what his inheritance ever was, and then, and then . . . colon cancer?

A reversal on Forrest Gump, here a brilliant guy brought down. No fat-bellied Middle American platitudes that the '60s were our misfortune. Like a forty-four caliber hollow-tipped bullet through the heart of the comfortable revisionism and out the other side comes the man who could lead us all.

And Bush, who had his nose in the air like a priss over Bill Clinton, cringes when he sees who's coming. The jig is up, in a certain way. The prissy probity gives way to a nervous grin.

But I feel I have no right to say more than what happened. Or more truthfully, I'm scared to.

\*

We fall from grace early, we products of the great American meritocracy. I'm sure I half-forget how snobbish we were, how ambitious, how unfair, our lack of mercy and dumb labels and casual little crudities. Our shortsightedness, too. We were nearly blind.

But compared to today, when perhaps we see more but all the colors are gray?

# CHAPTER 16

Harry sat on the gurney with his legs dangling down, so oblivious to the nurses attending to his cuts they could have stitched his lips shut and he might not have noticed. The rest of us stood around in the bath of fluorescent light like the accident victims we were. I felt a growing nausea, for the altered, cramped dimensions of things. I felt claustrophobic, as if Sascha and Harry had been holding the tent of the world up and now it was fallen down in suffocating shreds. None of us said anything. The surgeon, Cairns, came through, with his head down and papers in his hand, grimacing, in a hurry to get to a desk. The wall clock said a quarter to seven, a colorless dawn mounted the storm-streaked windows. The nurses were done with Harry. He hardly seemed to notice. He still sat there, and then Bloch came back.

He shut the door with such quiet exactitude it seemed to bring even more attention to himself, to how hard he was trying not to disturb. He looked almost serene, as though he'd gone out and given himself a good talking-to. I caught Harry's look. Studied neutrality. He told me later he dreaded to hear Bloch's voice then, he thought he should just walk out.

But for myself, I began to feel something like pity for Bloch. He seemed like an old tragic actor wearing too much makeup. The Great Bloch, Bloch the Magnificent. Probably what I felt was a lot less than pity; more like a generalized inclination, if "a" and "b" and "c" were so, to cut the guy a little slack. Pity being way over my head, pity being something a kid read about and never quite understood. But I saw it then in Cord too. Mixed with a little bit of gristly fear that Bloch might have gone over some sort of cliff and we didn't want our hands on it.

Bloch rolled his lips together. His hands were in the pockets of his jacket. He came up to Harry, unblinking, maybe hoping or half-expecting Harry to say something first, but he didn't.

Bloch seemed defenseless then. Throwing his dirtbag self on the mercy of the court.

And what if there had been a deer? This idea dawned on me. Maybe I hadn't seen everything. Maybe it had been there darting and leaping, at an angle or a depth in the fog I couldn't see, and Bloch swerved because he had to swerve because it was worse if you hit the deer.

I still didn't think there'd been a deer, but I wasn't sure now.

"If there was something in the world I could do to change this . . ." His words felt rehearsed, yet there was hoarse, groaning feeling in them.

"Me too," Harry said.

"I told Louie. I told these guys. I can barely speak . . ."

Harry nodded.

"I'm so sorry," Bloch said.

But he didn't back off or bow his head. Instead he stared at Harry, and he still didn't blink.

"Please don't stare at me," Harry said. "I'm not a freak."

"I'm not either."

"Nobody said you were," I said.

"Why would they have to?"

"Oh come on, Adam," Teddy said. "Self-pity's not the thing right now."

"Self-pity? *Me*?"

"No, not you," Cord said. He spoke so softly it seemed at first the inflection of his courtesy, but it was really his desperation. "We're just trying to get by here," he muttered. "Nobody's blaming you."

"Of course you are," Bloch said. "Of course you are. What a joke! What hypocrisy! You're all hypocrites! This is bullshit!" Bloch broken open, his hoarseness like a wound, his secret life pouring out like dark unaerated blood. "*I* killed her? Are you saying *I* did? I had to drive you home, okay? Who asked you to get drunk? Drunk pieces of shit!"

"Adam, calm down," Teddy said.

"I *am* calm. Can't you see? I'm calm. Calm. Calm Adam Bloch, cool under pressure, all the grace in the world under pressure. So fuck you, alright? *You* calm down. I was driving in fucking fog, I saw a fucking deer, I tried to miss it, I did my fucking best, alright? That's not good enough? I didn't try to kill us all! I didn't try to kill her!"

The fluorescent hum again. The murmurs of our hearts.

Bloch shifted his weight, glared at the floor with a kind of willed focus, as if looking at Harry again was forbidden so the floor, in spite, would became his self-imposed exile.

Harry asked Cord if he had any change and we all went into our pockets, almost comically, like guys in a forties movie when a pretty girl asks for a light and they all pull out their Zippos.

J. Lewis

A quarter, a packet of pretzel sticks from the vending machine. Harry chewed through the cellophane but then he couldn't eat any of the contents and passed the packet around and we couldn't eat either.

Bloch too waved it away. Downturned head. No thanks. Bloch's breath heaving. Harry dumping the pretzels in the trash, angrily, first crushing the packet in his fist.

"You don't even know I exist." For being so hoarse, his throat in every syllable, Bloch's voice was almost gentle now. "None of you do, not even you, Harry. Not really. I only exist so you can blame somebody. If somebody gets killed, it's Bloch who must have done it. There couldn't have been reasons. There couldn't have been a deer. It had to be the weenie flamer."

He looked at each of us again, by turns, a lawyer silently polling the jury.

"Adam, cut it out," I said.

"I loved her too, you know that? That ever occur to any of you? That's not possible, right? Adam Bloch, love somebody?"

He walked toward the door, his head down like Jacques Tati about to make a comic exit. Somehow he stuck an arm out and the door gave way, then we couldn't see him anymore.

I had a moment of almost tender wonderment. Bloch was right, it had never occurred to me, that he loved her too.

And those other things he said? What a terminal jerk, I must have thought.

You're no credit to your race, you terminal jerk, is what I must have thought.

George Washington Carver, a credit to his race. Adam Bloch, not.

But I still wondered about the deer.

We were a sea of anger and without Bloch there was no shore

to lap on. My claustrophobia returned. What could anyone say to Harry? Trash Bloch a little more? Why bother. Ask Harry if he wanted something, ask if we could help in any way? What a pious crock. Not worth bothering with that either.

The heavens must be very full, because the world was so empty.

I didn't believe that Sascha was dead. Or I believed it but only intermittently, what they say about stopped clocks, right twice a day.

We were all waiting for Harry to be the good daddy and tell us it was all alright.

But how do you comfort a good daddy? And how do you continue to believe such errant crap when the "good daddy" is struck down?

Silently, I struggled to find compassion for my friend.

And then he said he needed to make more phone calls.

Cord offered to go with him, stay with him, make some of the calls for him. But Harry didn't want that.

Of course he didn't.

In his absence we drank a little coffee and finally ate Oreos out of the vending machine. We were tired now. The hospital began to show signs of daytime life. At eight the shift would change, but by seven fifteen the nurses were sitting down more, doing their night's paperwork. My head buzzed and I ached to sleep. I was "thinking" of Sascha, which meant that I was thinking nothing at all, playing an elaborate mental hide-and-seek to keep away the feeling of her absence.

Cord asked one of the nurses where he was. She said he was in a room on the phone. Cord's forehead looked crinkled up, so I said, "It's only been fifteen minutes. Not even fifteen."

"More than fifteen," Teddy said.

J. Lewis

"Is it?" I said, though I knew it wasn't, I'd been glancing at my watch and anyway I always knew the time.

"Just seems long," Cord said.

"It is, it's been," Teddy said.

They were sitting in a row of plastic chairs and I was standing by them, so that we wouldn't be three in a row, so that we'd be tighter than that. "Did you go to that party?" Teddy said. His voice tailed off a little, as he remembered whatever it was he was going to say. He leaned forward and folded his hands. He was talking to Cord. "At the Field Club. Did you come down? When Deedee Winchester puked all over me?"

"You were such a gentleman," Cord said.

"Well for Christ sake."

"You didn't have to push her out of the car."

"I did *not* push her out of the car. I pushed her *head* out. So she wouldn't puke on the upholstery. Christ, you think I pushed her out of the car?"

"No Teddy, you were Mr. Chivalry."

"She barfed on my jacket, my shirt, my pants."

"She had the flu. She wasn't blotto or anything."

"The flu is no excuse for projectile vomiting in a grown female."

"Did you screw her?"

"Hell no. Jesus. . . . Remember Breed Phipps, hanging from the chandelier? That was the same party."

"What was that, fourth form?"

"I don't know. Was it?"

I didn't even try to say anything. Why would I? Their lives, or their once-upon-a-time lives. Mine was nowhere to be seen.

Teddy, never looking up, as though I wasn't there, continued on about Deedee and dry cleaning bills and Breed's parents having to pay eleven hundred dollars to fix the chandelier.

I thought of telling him he was starting to sound like Noel Coward, which would have pissed him off because even we knew Noel Coward was queer, but then he said, to Cord, "Sascha was there."

"She was?"

"She came late. She came with Alison Gardiner."

"I don't remember."

"You don't remember because you were off in the bushes doing the evil deed with Veronique, you vile-minded fuck."

"Definitely not the bushes in December."

"I'd gone home. I'd come back with clean clothes. I'd never met a girl from Brearley. Supposed to be brainy, all that shit, I gave her shit for that. Tony Garrison introduced us. You know him? He was from Greenwich. He went to Hotchkiss. . . . I danced with her three or four times."

"And?"

"And what? Did I put moves on her like a dirty-minded southern fuck undoubtedly would have?"

"Did you have a crush on her?"

"No. You know, I didn't. I liked her. But I was in love with somebody else at the time."

"Who?"

"Deedee Winchester."

I laughed. Funny turn, touching. But even my laughter didn't get an acknowledging glance from Teddy.

"Now it's been twenty minutes," I said.

"Maybe we should just go in there," Cord said.

"I didn't know you knew Sascha so long ago," I said to Teddy.

"It's been more like half an hour," he said to Cord.

I said again, in case he hadn't heard me, "I didn't know you knew Sascha so long ago."

"Something you don't know? Amazing," Teddy said.

"What do you mean?"

"Nothing. I don't mean anything, Louie."

"Teddy can be so charming," Cord said.

"Hey, if it's twenty minutes, it's twenty minutes, Louie says so."

"Teddy, Jesus," I said.

"Did it ever occur to you, Lou, that this whole thing's your fault?"

"Actually, about every other minute," I said.

"You think I'm kidding? What was that shit, you being so fucking smart, if you go to Vietnam because you want to get elected president, you can't do that. It's not pure enough. Who asked you?"

"Nobody."

"So great, so Mr. Knows-every-fucking-thing, if you didn't say that to her, she wouldn't've gotten him upset, he wouldn't've gotten plowed. If he wasn't plowed, Bloch wouldn't've been driving."

"Teddy, shut up. You're being a total flamer," Cord said. "That's the stupidest thing I ever heard."

"Okay. I'm not saying it was a direct cause."

But he was.

"I'm not Bloch," I said.

"Who said you were?"

"You're acting like it. You're substituting me for him."

"Don't be paranoid."

"*Me*, paranoid? Cord's right. This is bullshit."

The nurse came back to say Harry wasn't in any of the rooms. The other nurse, who heard this, said she'd seen him go outside, she thought he was looking for our other friend.

We went out to the parking lot but Harry wasn't there. The squall with Teddy lingered sullenly over us, he wasn't talking to me and I didn't know what to say to him, so Cord said, "We better split up. We better look for them." The morning was starting overcast and cold. We seemed to be the only ones around.

From the parking lot there was a road that went into the village and a dirt track that seemed like it might go to the water. Cord and I took the track. It was a crooked little track overhung with birch and spruce and posted with No Trespassing signs. At the water's edge were gravelly mud and beslimed rocks and a seascape of low tide, mottled grays, and calm. A cormorant made its low Spruce Goose takeoff from the water. Our visibility in either direction down the shore was limited by outreaches of land. Across the bay was nothing but forest and quiet shingle houses curtained by the spruce. There was no one in view anywhere, so we split up again, Cord moving north toward the village and I to the south.

A partial path snaked into the trees, but I was afraid it wouldn't continue to hug the waterline so I left it and made my way over the rocks and oozing mussel beds, my legs soaked almost to my knees and my pants like heavy flaps. I came around the first point of land and looked down the bay but there was another point directly south and the shoreline became steep and abrupt, so I had no visibility.

I scrambled over boulders, cutting my hands on the barnacles. My legs were freezing, my bandages fell off, the palms of my hands and my fingers stung from the salt water and barnacles. I felt like I was on a mission, driven by a rush of bitter resentment so profound I had scarcely felt it since my parents split apart. The fuck had Teddy been talking about? It just showed, it really did. When I loved people, it got messed up. Jesus, when I even *liked* people. And all this "we" shit I'd embellished. The boy runs shivering and alone. The "we" busted back into its atoms. All I wanted to do was find Harry. Or Bloch.

Out in deeper water I could see the staid, duck-like torso of a lobster boat puttering out, so indifferent to the drama I'd defined for myself that I thought it floated in a parallel world. I reached the second point of land, crawled up the scruffy grass to the top of it, and then I could see, two hundred yards to the south, a rickety pier like a bridge to oblivion and at the end of it two human shapes.

It appeared as if they were sitting at the end of it, their legs dangling off, as Harry had sat on the nurses' gurney in the hospital.

Quickly I covered half the ground between us. I waved but they weren't looking my way. I kept climbing over rocks. As soon as I could I began to run.

I was almost to the pier when Harry saw me. I hadn't shouted but he turned my way. Again I waved. It seemed to make no impression on him, as if his eyes were fixed on something more distant. He again looked out into the bay. I mounted the pier. For a few moments I felt in the creaking boards under my feet a kind of overlay, of another pier, or something like a pier, possibly the Playland boardwalk on Long Island Sound near where we'd lived before upstate and my parents' divorce, and at the end of it, awaiting my tentative, halting steps . . . who? My father? My mother? Both of them in the same picture, two stars in rare conjunction, looking slightly down in my direction, as if I was just beginning to walk?

Harry got up from the damp boards on the pier, brushed off the seat of his pants. Casually he looked my way. I had trouble reading his expression at first, but that was really because he hadn't one then. A little unslept, a little hungover. Otherwise he was just Harry. As if all the sorrow, the tragedy, now resided within him, he'd swallowed them whole as the whale swallowed Jonah.

Bloch got up too. He had a bloated look and he was starting to look unshaven and he didn't look my way. I thought he was looking past me. I turned to see if Teddy or Cord were there but they were not.

Bloch was still looking past me. I thought he was crazy on account of it.

Harry said, "I forgive him."

Bloch didn't even blink.

For a moment my only feeling was the rage I'd carried from town. Bloch was standing beside Harry like a friend. There was no space between them, only inches, as though they could smell each other's breath.

I could have mouthed the words then, some formula, some piling on top of Harry's, "I forgive you too, Adam," mumbled or muttered or oddly without affect like a defendant's confession at a show trial. But Harry must have known where I'd be going. "Wait," he said. "Wait till, you know—I can't say it, Louie. You'd have the words."

"Find it in my heart?"

"I knew you'd have the words."

But I didn't think I really did, and maybe he didn't either.

He looked so normal. He looked like nothing had happened at all but the end of a late summer idyll, a slightly wrecked weekend in the country.

I knew my rage was finished then. It had nowhere to go. The same spirit that forgave Bloch accepted me. There was not one without the other. Take it all or leave it all. I'd ridden in with Harry Nolan and I would ride out with him, or I would ride out alone. His girl, his gang of guys, his big ruling spirit, his catastrophe. If he wanted to forgive Bloch, who was I to say?

At last Bloch looked at me. "There wasn't any deer," he said, and I nodded.

\*

And later in Blue Hill we found Cord and Teddy, exhausted, on the steps of the old white church. Teddy got up when he saw me coming. He had an odd, surprised expression, as if he needed to make sure we weren't ghosts. I was a little surprised when he began to weep profusely. He puts his arms around me in particular, and his thin frame shook as he wept.

# CHAPTER 17

In one of the letters I received from Ft. Ord, Harry told me what happened with him and Bloch. Even today, when time has licensed me to carry a more jaundiced view of the world, I take what he wrote for about how it was.

He went out looking for him because like the rest of us he didn't want him on his conscience. He was prepared to lie like hell, to say anything at all, so that Bloch wouldn't do something stupid. He didn't want to have to think about Bloch anymore. That was it, really. He wished the world, or rather his mind, was clean of him. He wished, from his soul's point of view, that Bloch be extinct. But that would never happen if Bloch threw himself in front of a car or whatever else he could think of.

As well, Harry was trying to run away from Sascha. Not from her spirit, which he posited elsewhere, but her body, lying without dignity, confusing and challenging to everything he was willing himself to believe, an outrage, in some white sterilized room of the same building. It was driving him crazy.

He struggled to think instead of all the things Bloch had said in his tantrum if that's what it was. The fucking fog, the fucking deer, his fucking best. He couldn't even curse right. Bloch couldn't. Too many fuckings, too much pleading. He sounded like a bitch.

The first place Harry went looking was the bay because on reflection where else would Bloch go, Bloch who was afraid of the water, who'd worn his life jacket all day long. It took but ten minutes to find him, Bloch standing at the end of the pier as if in position for some darkly plotted version of an Olympic dive. That is to say, he was facing away from the land, with the toes of his shoes over the edge of the boards, and every little while he looked nervously down, at the slushy water or his shoes.

Which was all, grotesquely, like one of the experiments in the course on fear and courage that Harry had taken from Donald Webber, the one who flew him down to Millbrook. Yale had a new building for art and architecture then, it was the cat's pajamas of its time but it was not yet complete, so that it was possible to sneak around the scaffolding at night and climb up to the flat roof and put your feet half over the edge and stare down a hundred and fifty feet at the tops of cars and beckoning asphalt and write a paper on your findings. It was not only possible, it was required. Bloch was also taking that class, it was there that Harry met him. Bloch had been florid in the paper he wrote, he had recorded every millimeter of fear in his body, he had been a poet of fear.

But the tide was out now, and if Bloch had jumped he might have hit his head or broken a leg but he would not have drowned. Or it would not have been easy to drown, after he jumped he would still have had to want to drown, or he might have been knocked unconscious.

The water at the end of the pier covering the rocks was, by Harry's guess and depending which rock you stood on, four or five feet deep. Harry walked out on the rotting planks toward Bloch. He called so as not to scare him. Bloch said nothing but by the time Harry was close he had turned around. Now his heels were at the edge of the boards, as if keeping contact with the edge for safety's sake, or assurance of escape, the way some people will only live on the coast. Harry stayed six feet away, didn't want to crowd him.

"Hey."

"Hey."

"So. What's going on?"

"You care?"

Harry's shrug.

"You must hate me."

"Maybe."

"I want you to hate me."

"That's horseshit, Adam."

Bloch turned his back on Harry, his feet pivoting around but still working the edge.

Harry thought, he wants me to push him over, he wants me to do it for him. And he hated Bloch even more. The masochist says hit me, the sadist says no. But he hated Bloch so much then that he really wanted to do it. How hard would it be? A tap in the middle of the back and he would fall. Harry even looked up and down and around like a burglar casing a block. No one. He didn't give a shit. His caution was gone.

But then he remembered the shallowness of the water. Bloch would be standing on a rock with a couple of bruises and freezing and he'd wind up jumping in to save him.

Then he hated him that much more. "Turn around, Adam. This is pathetic."

"What is?" Still turned away.

"Your self-dramatizing shit. You can call attention to yourself as much as you want, it's not going to change anything. It's not going to make you a better person. It's not going to bring her back."

So Bloch turned around and faced him, and took a shuffling step away from the edge, and then, according to Harry, he hated Bloch still more. He hated his brown pleading eyes, his hair, the hoarseness of his voice, his thick eyebrows, the way he stood there like a round dumb stone when he was not. In fact he hated that he was smart. He hated that he had thought everything out. He hated that he wasn't afraid to jump.

Because Harry knew that now: Bloch was not afraid to hurt himself, and if he was still afraid to die, he was not afraid enough.

"I, uh . . ." Bloch fished around for words in a way that seemed at first like it wasn't real but it was. "I don't think I saw a deer." He blinked. "No, that's not right. There wasn't. There just wasn't. I'm certain of it. I wasn't falling asleep exactly. But I got confused by the fog. . . . There wasn't a deer."

Harry saw that there was no more pleading in Bloch's eyes. He had given up. He was like a bag of flesh and bone. Harry didn't mean to forgive him then. It wasn't anything he tried to do. But Bloch was as good as naked. Harry felt the urge to throw clothes around him, as if he'd just been lifted from the sea, lips chattering and blue.

And he stared at Bloch so hard that the outlines of his body seemed to vibrate, then grew diffuse, as though what was Bloch and what was the world were no longer clear.

Harry wrote me that as he stared at this sack of flesh and bone, Bloch seemed to him no more nor less a part of the world than the ocean. Would Harry blame a drop of water? Would he blame a fish?

If Bloch had fault, the world had fault.

And was Harry himself a part of the world? He felt the bitter parchedness in his mouth turn to sweet plentiful saliva, as if he had a taste for Bloch, as if he was about to eat him. The carnivore loves his prey, the cannibal has his reasons.

Harry and Bloch and the fish and the carnivore and the prey and the cannibal and the cannibal's reasons and all the fault of the world swimming in the same ocean.

Harry forgave Bloch, in a sense, because he didn't want to piss himself.

Though it was really a movement of his heart as much as his mind. His heart, unspeaking, swimming in the world.

Those last words are mine, not Harry's. I apologize to him for getting fancy.

He had hated Bloch out of existence. What was left was purified, the end product of futility.

He walked toward Bloch and put his hands on his shoulders. Bloch looked at him with a kind of acceptance, beyond fear or humility, a gazelle showing her neck.

Harry was inches from Bloch, so close that Adam's face seemed like a landscape of sorrows, fought over, pitted, abandoned.

Harry, leaning forward, felt on his lips the brittleness of Bloch's dark stubble. Bloch was poised, frozen, as if for death. Harry kissed his cheek.

"You're a fucking asshole like the rest of us," Harry said.

Bloch blinked away silent tears. Harry felt their dampness on his cheek as he withdrew.

A few minutes later they were sitting side by side with their legs dangling down, looking out at the cormorants on the bay. Somewhere in there Bloch repeated what he'd said before, "I'm so sorry." Harry said nothing. The alchemy was over. He was thinking only of Sascha again. A little while later I found them.

*

An alternative version of Sascha's death. With her out of the way I danced with Harry. I was a terrible dancer but he swept me around the room. I dreamed this once. And in this scenario what is Bloch but the new bitch on the block?

I also dreamed that I forgave Bloch, his face was big and square, we were somewhere that was near a carousel, in a park in Italy, in a black-and-white film on a Sunday afternoon, and I felt the idiocy of not forgiving him, because here I was and here he was, and I said to him, "This is all Harry's fault. This is his miracle. If I can forgive you, that's really something." "Are you doing it because Harry made you?" Bloch said. "*Made* me? Don't be ridiculous," I said. "Then he inspired you." "I told you, it was a miracle, what more do you want from me?" And then Bloch said, "I forgive you too," and I thought that was ridiculous but very sporting of him. We bought tickets for the merry-go-round and paid in lire, of which I had a wad, and after that I didn't remember.

*

Another alternative version of Sascha's death. She is an angel. She is my muse. She flies close over our heads.

*

To my knowledge, Harry never mentioned again not going in the army.

# CHAPTER 18

There wasn't much in the papers. The bare details. A car crash. Where she went to school and who her parents were and her husband's name.

I don't know what was in the *Harvard Crimson*. Probably the same.

One thing about dying in a car crash when you're twenty-two and newly married is that you probably never talked about where you want to be buried. She hadn't exactly, but on the other hand they had talked about where Harry wanted to be buried if he died in the service. It was a conversation you had if you were young and sincere with each other and Harry had said California, by the Pacific, by a surfer beach. But now it was she who was dead and there was no question she would have wished to be near him, and yet her family didn't want her so far away and "alone." Harry didn't hesitate. It's where you were when you were alive that counted. Of course, we say. Of course.

There was a graveyard on Mount Desert Island near the Maclarens' summer homes. I say homes plural because several of the family had places scattered around, their estates like British colonial pink on the local maps. The graveyard was on a rocky rise near the sea. On a good day in August you might see whales breaching offshore, but this was September and the ocean was flat and empty.

The funeral was on Thursday. Harry's father's office had made the phone calls and his induction was delayed until Tuesday. They would have given him two weeks but he didn't want it, he didn't know what he would do with the time, he wanted to get on with it.

I spent a little while with him the morning of the service. We walked along a ridge by the water. He was as solemn and measured and composed as I'd ever known him to be. But I remember the tiredness of his eyes. Harry's eyes had never been tired. He said to me, "She really loved you, you know that, Louie. She talked about you. Of all our friends."

"No, I didn't know that," I said.

"Poor fucking taste on her part, if you ask me," he said.

"Anyway she didn't *love* me," I said.

"Okay, she *liked* you. That more comfortable?"

"What did she say about me?"

Harry shrugged. "I don't know. Just things. Things she liked. She liked that you were smart. The way you talked to her. . . . You know, it could have turned out like *Jules and Jim*."

"I don't think so."

"No really. She would have gone to you for stability. She needed both. She needed me but she also needed, or she would have . . . someone like you."

"You're making that up."

"She would have left you, of course."

"Yeah, of course." Sarcastic.

"Shit! Stick up for yourself! Jesus! When are you going to grow up? You had to fight me for her, you fuck!"

"I hate to lose."

"Next time you fight."

"What next time?"

"You'll have one."

We walked along the ridge.

"Just remember, you jumped on the harbor bell," he said.

"That was slightly stupid, wasn't it?" But I smiled.

"I did it. You did it."

We walked along. I kept my eyes close to the ground because I was too full of feeling to put them anyplace else.

"When do you leave for Greece?"

"A couple weeks."

"I'm not going to let this kill me. She'd kill me if I did," Harry said.

"She would," was all I said.

Then the service in a stone Episcopal chapel. Hymns and prayers and no testimonies. The interment of her ashes in the spare, lovely graveyard. Familiar faces from the wedding in June, all sensing it was about sixty years too soon for this, surprised, shaken, wounded, their chattering and laughter now become a dark mirror image of shadow and silence, like a film turned into its negative.

I had trouble listening to the words of the prayers. My mind flew off, replayed a hundred scenes, but what it did not do was think of the future.

Teddy and Cord were beside me, the three of us standing behind the white rows of chairs, lined up as if we were still the ushers at the wedding. They owned dark suits, the best I could do was gray. Adam Bloch was not there.

I watched, as much as I watched anything, the back of Harry's head. He was the one who carried the box of ashes to the gravesite. As he did this I thought of his crewcut and of the crash and of where Adam Bloch was now, and I heard the word "God" pass through my mind like a cloud and I tried to picture Sascha at a moment when her downturned mouth turned up but I had trouble picturing her at all and I wondered, if everyone's mind wandered like mine, who there would be to mourn her.

What is mourning? I don't think it's being sad, or any single feeling of grief. I think it's when your whole world darkens a little, as if the power supply has been cut by a certain percent, as if the universe is showing its respect.

We went to her parents' summer house afterward, a sprawling white clapboard cottage of loose-limbed charm with lawns down to the water. Sounds like a real-estate blurb but there it was. I stayed only a little while. Harry was busy with the family. We spoke briefly again, inconsequentially. I gave him the address of my school in Greece. We hugged and I felt the enormous muscular solidity of his body. He must have been twice as big around as I. He said watch your ass with the greasers. He went inside because someone was on the phone, one of Sascha's friends had gotten lost trying to find the graveyard. I said good-bye to everybody and left.

\*

*From Pvt. Harry Nolan, #28299754, class 29A, Co. C-1BN-5BDE,*
*Fort Ord, Calif., November 12, 1966:*

Dear Louie,

Do NOT, if you can possibly help it, go in the Army. You will not like it.

The only saving grace of military life is that the Army seems to think it's come so far in turning me into one son-of-a-bitch of a killing machine that they've promoted me to "acting sergeant."

This is outstanding, it frees me from all details, gives me the advantages of rank, and challenges me just enough to pass the time. I'm in charge of sixty men, most of them draftees, and feelings can get rather vehement against the old Ivy League. But they're not bad guys. Really they're pretty great. One's a total ringer for Doberman.

Speaking of Ivy League, you hear anything about Brian Dowling? This guy is good. And Calvin Hill? Whoa! But I'm betting you don't get too much Yale football coverage in the Salonica newspaper. For that matter, they don't give a fuck in the SF Chronicle either.

Cord's written twice. Hates his business school classmates, but likes Wharton, even likes Philadelphia. Conceivable explanation? He's got a girl, Leslie, junior at Penn. Further details not forthcoming. You know the winged wonder is a bit of a discreet tight-mouth. He did tell me about Teddy, though. Which is good because that lazy dick hasn't written me himself. But he's officially P.C. now, he's arrived in Peru, he's assigned to some village in the Andes, and they've already managed to nearly blow up a whole mountain with dynamite. By mistake. The natives must love them. Also heard from Fred Singleton. Remember Freddy? He's already in Nam. USAID. He was asking if I was interested. I guess loanouts happen all the time. But I don't know.

As for the rest . . . And I guess you know what I'm talking about . . . I don't know, Louie. I think about her constantly. No matter what I'm doing, running, doing push-ups, ordering these clowns around, reading a book. I can't even read a book. Even getting shot at. Sometimes I wonder if I should just go get laid, maybe that would distract me for a little while. But I can't do that.

Time, they say. Time, lots of time. I guess I have lots of time. She ought to be with me now. That's my dogma. That's my one official belief. It's also all I can say about it for now.

Do you get the Herald Tribune over there? Maybe it was in there. The white fox made a speech in the Senate, questioning Westmoreland, questioning the whole thing. Go, Dad! It's a start, anyway. Just got to keep Scoop Jackson and the guys from Douglas Aircraft from pissing in his ear.

Okay, so I'm an inarticulate, slightly illiterate and uncouth fuck, but I've done my bit. Now, Louie, you write me back. I am desperate for tales of sunshine and blue water and statues with mysterious smiles. All we've got here is shitty food and talk of war.

And keep your nose out of those hairy Greek armpits.

Harry

It was the first, and the only one of the four letters from Ft. Ord that I still have. It was written on an aerogram, one of those things you fold like origami and there's no envelope so the thing is lighter and cheaper. Until I pulled it out recently I hadn't seen an aerogram for years. Harry wrote with a fountain pen, in thick, squat blue strokes that were somehow like his body. A clear hand, young, and if I could speak of the four letters as a whole, his writing style was easy and fluid, as if the kinks were few from his feelings to his mind to his hand.

I was surprised to get even one letter from him. I was a lame correspondent myself. My handwriting would get crabbed and I would say only the barest things and feel that I had to copy the thing over before I sent it. His letters all reached me in Thessaloniki, where I was teaching high school kids English so they could get ahead in their world that we Americans were laboring energetically and sometimes clumsily to turn west. From my windows in the stone dormitory I could see Mount Olympus fifty miles away. Not a bad life, an easy interval on the road to law school, but the letters from Harry made my days.

As for the others, which arrived every month or so, in a rhythmed response to my own lame efforts, a common theme (aside from the one about Bloch) was how quickly Harry was turning against the war. The thing that had so exercised our weekend had nothing to do with it, was never mentioned. Too late for purity of intention. It was all politics now. Allard Lowenstein had reentered his life. Lowenstein's new project was to find a peace candidate to run against Johnson in sixty-eight. Harry lobbied him for RFK but it was too early for that big play and eventually Lowenstein settled on Gene McCarthy. I don't doubt it was Lowenstein's influence that pushed Harry so quickly to an antiwar stance. But also a lot of his recruited buddies were black, and they were quiet but if you pressed them none-too-thrilled about the war. Harry was getting a first-hand look through the reverse end of the meritocratic telescope, where it was as plain as clap in the morning (his phrase, not mine) that the same policy that made safe harbors for the "best" so we'd be there to lead and preach and invent and administer in the future put others, maybe not expendable but simply less valuable, squarely in harm's way.

Not that even I wasn't playing my sweet, cosseted part in the Cold War effort. The school where I taught was private and plaques commemorating its largest, mostly American, donors lined the administration building's front hall. Sometime early in the year, two of its patrons were exposed as CIA fronts. I wrote Harry about my contributions protecting NATO's southern flank, more in irony than anything else, but I don't think he was amused.

He was smoking marijuana by then and was the first person I heard, by at least a year, to call it dope. Always a quick study. He made it to the Sierras finally, on the long weekend at the end of his advanced firearms school. I was so happy when I read that, in the last letter I received. He hiked alone the whole time in Kings Canyon park, he caught a seventeen-inch German brown trout and decided that if Sascha were alive he would have gotten her pregnant that weekend. He didn't seem unhappy. He seemed to be playing his hand.

The letters stopped. I assumed he had bigger things on his mind.

Then, too, I might not have received a letter. There was a coup in Greece in March. The rightist colonels who took over had all the savoir faire of Chaplin's little dictator. They banned mini-skirts, cut the hair of foreign hippies, and censored the mail coming in from abroad. They were a nasty lot, really. Fathers of my students were arrested and tortured. On the night of the coup itself an old Greek philologist at our school actually played Chaplin films to our students, who were confined by martial law to the hilltop campus overlooking the city, and he too was arrested. Then there was the young American diplomat whom we post–Ivy League teaching fellows had admired for his silky, amiable manner and the fact that he played squash every week with the king. The *New York Times* soon enough exposed him as the supposed American contact man for the coup. It seemed no matter where we went in the world in 1967 those of us who thought we were dancing on velvet saw the iron underneath.

I entered Harvard Law School in the fall. Bill Weld was in my class, and Mark Green who would lose spectacularly in a mayor's race in New York. More fodder for the mill. I thought law school would be a lot like college but it was not. No one had time to be friendly or nuts or scary or funny or anything that had any character to it anymore. My classmates with a few memorable exceptions were a stony bunch, as focused as a Zeiss lens and scarcely troubling to hide their ambitions, like a phalanx of Adam Blochs. And this was despite the collapse, the hippie-ization, of student life going on all around us. Some of this, but surprisingly little, wore off. Too many had invested too much. When Harvard College struck, it was at least roughly speaking for world peace and democracy. When the law school struck, it was because law students felt sorry for themselves, unable to study enough because of the local turmoil, and demanding pass/fail grades and no finals to ease their burdens.

The last thing I received from Harry was a postcard from Vietnam. Or it wasn't a postcard, it came in an envelope, it was a photograph the size of a postcard showing Harry filling sandbags. He had a shovel in his hand, his shirt was off, his crewcut was just as always, and he was laughing at the camera. He had a suntan and his boots were muddy. There were a couple of black guys also in the frame, leaning on their shovels and smoking cigarettes, and some sort of structure sat in the background. Nothing identified the place. On the back of the photograph he'd written, as if it were a postcard, "Hey Louie! You fucking prophet!"

When I heard, it was from Senator Nolan himself. I guess he was going down a list. His voice was like worn-out sandpaper. "Harry always spoke highly of you."

He was on short time, eleven days to go. He came under enemy attack and died at Thong Bon Tri, near Hue, February 10, 1968, while assisting a wounded soldier to a medevac helicopter.

# CHAPTER 19

An alternative version of Harry's death. Trumpets sound, as Shiva rejoins Parvati after an unbearable absence.

Another alternative version of Harry's death. There is none. More than three decades have passed and I have no words.

# CHAPTER 20

The fall I started law school I attended a series of lectures Borges gave to the university on the craft of poetry. I remember the slow movements of the frail blind man and the hushed reverence of the crowds that filled Memorial Hall and the steady, sly cadence of his voice, breaking each phrase with a little pause, as if everything were on an equal plane of mystery and discovery. But I couldn't remember anything in particular that he said until recently someone gave me a copy of those lectures on compact disc. I've been using the CDs to go to sleep at night. I find the reediness of Borges's voice comforting, and still being a meliorist, or maybe self-improvement addict is the better phrase, I keep imagining I might learn something in my sleep. But one thought of his has kept me awake. He was referring to the familiar lines of Robert Frost, "And miles to go before I sleep, / And miles to go before I sleep," and he said everything suggested is better than anything laid down. He quoted Emerson to the effect that arguments convince nobody. And Borges said the reason this is so is that when people hear an argument, they treat it like an argument, they turn it over and weigh it and they may decide against it. Whereas for something merely hinted at there is a kind of hospitality in our imagination, we're ready to accept it.

What keeps me awake is the thought that I may have put a sort of argument not too far from my book's heart.

Would Harry Nolan have been the American president if he had lived? I could say "of course not" and "probably not" or be preposterously optimistic and contentious on the subject, but the truth is without gravity, gone. Even if he had lived and persevered into a career, a score of things might have tripped him or turned his path. A close election loss somewhere or a brush with the law or a second wife who abhorred politics or a third who was Italian and took him off to Rome or the tilt of the country to the right while he continued left, or somehow, conceivably, a sex scandal, say, if it involved an illegitimate child—but nothing would have brought Harry Nolan down easily. If he had wanted to run in California, there are Democrats in high office who might be practicing mergers-and-acquisitions law today or be auditioning as Buddhist monks.

Though that's something else that might have stopped Harry. Becoming a Buddhist monk. Entering a monastery. Returning to Vietnam, or Cambodia, or Thailand.

It's hard to say. It's easy to list the obstacles. And yet.

I can see him up there where Bush is now. Someone who could see both sides of things. Or many sides of things, someone who could laugh at the scandal-mongers and yahoos and get away with it, who would rally the center and make it huge and yet be idiosyncratic and daring, and large-spirited in such a way that the word itself would not get used for propaganda. A president for war if need be but also a peace president, looking to the future with zesty favor, embracing the hurtling, contradictory world. A counterphobe, a guy who would run at fear and overwhelm it.

We all want a good daddy to be president. But why do we so seldom get one?

Or to put it another way, coming back to my generation.

And leaving aside for a moment the issue of Harry Nolan, my friend Harry Nolan, my likely prejudiced presentation on his behalf. Let us say it wasn't Harry Nolan, let's say it was someone else, from the nearly sixty thousand who were killed in Vietnam, or from the scores of thousands who went to Canada or jail or into hiding or otherwise removed themselves from the circle of public possibility. It's not about sides, it's not about who owns history.

I suspect that our generation may not have produced its greatest leaders because the best of us are gone. Or many of our best, anyway. Enough to make a difference, enough to have worsened the odds. We know from other times and places that great wars do this to nations, but we scarcely think of Vietnam that way out of a reluctance to remember that it was a great, omnivorous war, it swallowed up the country. Wasn't it just a dirty little colonial war, we say, a dirty little colonial war that still dirtier resisters turned into something big? Were the casualties really so many?

Maybe not. It depends how you count, I suppose.

But I do know this. We were and probably still are a predominantly Christian country. And in a predominantly Christian country there's very little to prevent the best going first. No membrane, no web of social relations or propriety is there to catch them. All the rules are built for those who would take advantage of them, hypocrites among them but anyway lesser men, not for those who would take no advantage at all. It's like a tragic law, of self-sacrifice.

Those who fought with pure hearts and courage, on one side or the other. All those who went over the edge. All those who stuck their necks out. Don't you do it, I'll do it. Good-bye.

Ghosts, dead or alive, calling out to us from Asia or Canada or the hills of Vermont or Oregon, or the graveyards.

The tremendous promise of our generation, carelessly lost, squandered.

And the guys who do get elected, our guys but not our best guys, do their best to hold the banner up. To be worthy, in a darkened world.

The funny thing is, I believe George Bush must know what happened to Harry Nolan. He probably vaguely remembers the whole story, Harry's promise, Harry and Sascha, Sascha's death, and Harry's. But what he thinks about any of it, I cannot imagine.

Is this an argument? Or is it only a hint, after all?

\*

A cold day in March. Once again, the graveyard on Mount Desert Island. The wind bit our faces and snapped the legs of our pants. The white fox of the west was there, and Harry's mother, and his sister whom I had never met, a big-boned woman then serving in the Peace Corps in Melanesia. Sloan Coffin was there. Allard Lowenstein was there. A black guy who was out of the service now but had been with Harry somewhere along the line was there. Adam Bloch was there. Sascha's mother and father and sister and brother were there. A few guys from DKE. A hundred others whom I couldn't identify. Cord and I were there, and Teddy who got leave from the Peace Corps to attend.

Words of caution from Sloan Coffin, followed by words of grief, then words of glad thankfulness. He used the word *glory*.

The hole already dug near Sascha's low stone. The ashes under a cloth, in a box, on a table beside the makeshift podium. Sloan Coffin's thinning hair flying around. All of us freezing, our toes rigid.

A few of us had asked to speak.

Allard Lowenstein went first. He mentioned that time in Mississippi where Harry had shut him down. In his rendering Harry was more like the agonized apprentice afraid to go against his mentor but finally getting up the guts. It felt unfamiliar, oddly refracted, but then Allard recalled a time when Harry had finally gone against his father, over some bill that had money in it for the Phoenix program, which meant assassinations in Vietnam, and Harry had called up Washington from Da Nang and given his father hell. And that part felt real enough. Lowenstein never knew Sascha.

Then it was our turn, Teddy and Cord and I. We had asked to speak together, but now there was a minor hitch. We conferred with Reverend Coffin. Would it be possible to speak once the ashes were in the ground? He was not a formal person and he didn't see why not.

Senator Nolan placed the ashes of his only son in the earth. He wept openly.

Sloan Coffin read the twenty-third psalm.

I saw the whitecaps on the ocean and I thought I saw a whale, but it was as illusory as Bloch's deer.

We sang *The Battle Cry of Freedom* and everyone knew the words and it wasn't a dream this time.

Then a few others asked to speak and this went on awhile, Harry's sister Susan spoke and she was strong and funny and

Sascha's mother who was unspeakably sad, and a coach from St. Paul's, and an aunt.

Until it was our turn again. Despite the cold I had begun to sweat. We meant to be short and sweet, Teddy told the crowd.

We had made this pledge, Cord said, and Harry was holding us to it.

The three of us turned around in poorly choreographed disunity and unzipped our flies. I was afraid I would not be able to piss on account of the cold, I was sweaty and my neck was stiff from embarrassment. I managed only a dribble at first, which flew back with the wind against my pants. Teddy and Cord got theirs going easily, and slowly my stream grew stronger, as I realized there was nothing left to lose. Soon all of us were watering Harry's ashes, the best we could anyway, the box and the muddy hole they sat in.

When we turned around we met horrific stares, but I felt sane and even proud.

Was there anyone on our side? Lowenstein, maybe, and a couple of the guys from DKE, whose eyes shone in recollection. I couldn't see Adam Bloch then. I didn't know where he had gone, or maybe he'd gone nowhere and I just didn't see him.

As we walked away, Senator Nolan approached me with a quizzical expression. "Symbolic speech," I said, and the white fox of the west smiled lightly through his tears.